PRAISE FOR WISHING FOR MISTLETOE

"Robin Lee Hatcher's *Wishing for Mistletoe* is a heartfelt romance perfect for the holidays. Her novel is my first visit to the fictional town of Sanctuary, and it's a delightful enticement to read the rest of the series. Her sweet love story is best enjoyed with a cup of hot choco-late and a Christmas cookie or two—and if you can arrange a snowfall, that would be perfect. I finished this satisfying blend of love and hope against the quaint back-drop of Sanctuary Island with a smile on my face." — Beth K. Vogt, award-winning author of *Dedicated to the One I Love*

"Charming and delightful with all the feels you want in a Christmas novel, *Wishing for Mistletoe* is a must for your holiday reading." — Rachel Hauck, New York Times Best-selling author

"When I pick up a Robin Lee Hatcher novel, I know I will be entertained, but what I love most is that I'm also edified. Ariel's recognition of God's hand of guidance in her life, even in the challenging and painful moments, resonated with me long after I finished the story. And something else . . . Hatcher inspires me to believe in happily ever afters. *Wishing for Mistletoe* is a true delight from beginning to *ahh*-inducing end." — Kim Vogel Sawyer, bestselling author of *Bringing Maggie Home*

"If you're looking for a book to get you in the Christmas spirit, *Wishing for Mistletoe* will do the trick. When struggling Idaho author Ariel Highbridge arrives at quaint Sanctuary Island on Lake Huron to work on her next book, she meets her neighbor Tom Fuller and his young daughter Shauna. Unable to write, Ariel turns back to God as she grows closer to the widower and his daughter. Has the Lord brought her here for a reason, or just a season? This sweet story of faith and family touched my soul. The obstacles against Tom and Ariel were real, but their faith and the Christmas spirit brought them together. Grab your mug of hot chocolate and enjoy this story!" — Lenora Worth, NYT bestselling author

"In *Wishing for Mistletoe* a romance blossoms between a blocked author, retreating to Sanctuary Island for inspiration, and a widower who's uncertain about surrendering his heart again. Hatcher expertly weaves a gentle romance while exploring the role of faith in decisions both big and small. Grab a cozy blanket and snuggle up with this heart-warming, romantic tale!" — Denise Hunter, bestselling author of *Before We Were Us*

WISHING FOR MISTLETOE

A SMALL TOWN CHRISTIAN ROMANCE

LOVE ON SANCTUARY SHORES
BOOK SIX

ROBIN LEE HATCHER

Wishing for Mistletoe
by Robin Lee Hatcher
Copyright © 2024 RobinSong, Inc.
ALL RIGHTS RESERVED

Scripture quotations taken from the (NASB®) New American Standard
Bible®, Copyright © 1960, 1971, 1977, 1995, 2020 by The Lockman
Foundation. Used by permission. All rights reserved. lockman.org

Paperback ISBN: 978-1-962005-04-3
eBook ISBN: 978-1-962005-03-6

Library of Congress Control Number: 2024917104

Published by RobinSong, Inc.
Meridian, Idaho

"For I am convinced that neither death, nor life, nor angels, nor principalities, nor things present, nor things to come, nor powers, nor height, nor depth, nor any other created thing will be able to separate us from the love of God that is in Christ Jesus our Lord." (Romans 8:38–39, NASB 2020)

To the One who brings Joy to the World, at Christmas and all year through.

WELCOME TO SANCTUARY

I'm delighted you've chosen to read *Wishing for Mistletoe*. I hope you enjoy it. Just in case you didn't know, this novel is part of a multi-author series, Love on Sanctuary Shores, that includes these titles:

Tumbling into Tomorrow by Juliette Duncan
Fighting for Her Heart by Tara Grace Ericson
Surrendering to Love by Kristen M. Fraser
Running into Forever by Jennifer Rodewald
Trusting His Promise by Valerie M. Bodden
Wishing for Mistletoe by Robin Lee Hatcher

Happy reading,
Robin Lee Hatcher

CHAPTER 1

November

Ariel Highbridge pulled the hood of her coat tight at her throat as The Haven ferry plowed through the choppy waters of Lake Huron on its way to Sanctuary Island. By the end of November, ferry service would cease until spring, and the only way to reach the island would be by private boats—until ice formed on the surface of the lake—and small aircraft.

She shuddered, both from the cold and the thought of flying in one of those tiny planes. The cold she could live with. But she wouldn't go anywhere in a tin can with wings. The very idea gave her nightmares. No, once she was on the island, it would be her home for the next six months. Whatever else happened, the next time she stepped onto the mainland, it would be from the ferry.

"Shauna," a male voice called above the sound of the wind. "Come back inside."

Laughter drew Ariel's gaze to the side. She guessed the girl at the railing to be about ten or eleven years old. Although she wore a warm coat, gloves, and boots, her head was uncovered, and curly red hair blew around in the wind, like a sweater caught in a blender.

"Shauna. Come on."

"Just a second, Dad."

"Now, Shauna."

Shauna looked at Ariel and grinned. Almost as if they shared a secret.

Ariel smiled in return. "You'd better do as your dad says."

Shauna laughed again, whirled away from the railing, and ran toward the doorway to the passenger deck. Ariel caught only the back of the man's head as dad and daughter disappeared inside, the door closing behind them.

Her heart pinched as she remembered her own father. He'd had to summon her back from misadventures about a million times while she was growing up. How long-suffering he'd been with her as she'd pushed his boundaries, a little more every year. Life without him had never been the same, and the passing of a dozen years hadn't stopped her from wishing she could talk to him even one more time.

What would Charles Highbridge think of his only daughter if he could see her today? He'd been gone more than a decade now. Would he be proud or disappointed of the woman she'd become? What advice would he share with her if only he could?

"I miss you, Dad. I could sure use some advice right about now."

The harbor at Sanctuary Island drew closer. Toward the southeast side of the island, she saw the big resort hotel—the Shore View Palace—that drew tourists to Sanctuary throughout the summer. Beyond the dock where passengers would disembark from the ferry, she saw the small town of Sanctuary. Her friend, Gwyneth Muldoon, had told her no motorized vehicles were allowed within the five square blocks that made up the town proper. Residents walked or rode bicycles, and in the winter when snow blanketed the ground, they used skis and snowshoes. In season, tourists often went through the town in a horse-drawn carriage, stopping to visit shops and galleries.

With some creaks and groans and the growl of engines, the ferry slowed as it drew closer to the dock. Pushing the hood off her head, Ariel went inside the main deck to retrieve her briefcase and rolling suitcases.

Please, God, help me find my creativity again. Let this place be the answer. I don't have any others.

Fifteen minutes later, Ariel set foot on the dock and rolled her two suitcases through the open gates, past the ferry offices, across the road, and into town. Gwyneth's instructions were easy enough to follow: Once in town, continue on Main Street past the town square and go all the way to Sixth Street. Turn left and go two blocks.

Her friend's home was on the northwest corner of Superior and Sixth. A cream-colored house with red trim.

A chilly wind pushed against Ariel, and roiling clouds

threatened rain. She quickened her steps, eager to get inside before she got drenched. Despite her warm coat, she was shivering by the time she arrived at her destination. The house wasn't large, and it was definitely old. But it looked well cared-for. As fast as her icy fingers could manage, she retrieved the key from her purse and unlocked the front door.

She found the switch on the entry wall and flicked on the lights, providing her the first glimpse of what would be her home for the next six months, thanks to Gwyneth's generosity.

"I never visit the island in the off-season," her friend had told her. "You'll have the house all to yourself. And no tourists either. You'll have plenty of time to regroup and refresh. Not to mention you'll have few distractions. Unless you like to snowshoe or ski the trails."

Ariel had laughed at that. She wasn't a winter sports person. Winter was meant for warm fires, hot spiced apple cider, and a good book.

"And writing," she said aloud as she walked deeper into the house, turning on more lights as she went.

There were two bedrooms on the main floor. The larger one was decorated in hues of teal and mauve. Lovely and restful. The second bedroom was chintz from the wallpaper to the curtains to the bedspread and pillow shams. Even the framed prints on the wall. It was straight out of the 1950s and made Ariel smile. How like Gwyneth —who loved books and movies set in that era—to make such a choice.

While the chintz theme didn't spill into the living or

dining rooms, the home's furnishings made her think of her maternal grandparents' house in Boise. They'd purchased the home as newlyweds, and according to Ariel's mom, Grandma Dot hadn't changed a thing for the next fifty years. Ariel thought that an exaggeration, but her memories of the old house said it could be true. Her heart pinched, remembering the wonderful hours she'd spent with her grandmother as a little girl, baking cookies, helping in the garden. Grandma Dot, a widow of twenty-two years, had lost her battle with breast cancer twenty years ago and, like Dad, a hole had been left in Ariel's life with her passing.

Ariel continued her exploration of the main floor, checking out the tiny bathroom, the bright yellow kitchen, and a small laundry room. She took the time to study each of the framed photographs hanging in the hallway. Photos of Gwyneth at camp and after college graduation. Photos of her on a trip to England and Ireland. Fun photos with her family with everyone making a silly face at the camera. There was even one photo of Gwyneth and Ariel together outside a theater on Broadway in New York. What great memories.

Moving on, she discovered a third bedroom at the top of a set of steep and narrow stairs, although its true purpose seemed to be for storage.

By the time she returned to the living room, rain pelted the large window overlooking a small backyard. An ancient tree, bare of leaves, was in one corner with a rope-swing hanging from a gnarled limb. In the other corner of the yard stood a shed.

Although it was midday, the darkness of the storm

tempted her to curl up in the bed and take a nap. But she couldn't do that. She needed to unpack and settle in.

On her way to retrieve her suitcases from the front hall, she remembered Gwyneth had said she would leave a note with important information in the kitchen nook. She went into the kitchen and found the note, as promised.

Hi, Ariel. Welcome to Sanctuary. I hope it proves to be just that for you. A sanctuary.

My friend Tom Fuller lives right next door. If you need help of any kind, he's the one to call. He's very handy. Can fix most anything, and he loves to help. A really great neighbor. He's widowed with a young daughter, and when he isn't at school (he's a teacher), he's usually at his house. His number is on the pad next to the phone.

Another friend of mine promised to bring over enough food to get you through the next couple of days until you can stock up on what you want. Check the fridge and the cupboards.

Gwyneth's note then listed a couple of places to eat in the off-season as well as directions to the grocery store and the bookstore. What more could Ariel need? Right?

The furnace and water heater are in the half-basement. You get there by stairs outside. The fusebox is in the laundry room. There's a toolbox on the porch if you need a wrench or screwdriver or hammer. Extra lightbulbs are under the bathroom sink.

If there's anything I've forgotten to write down, you can always call me. Feel free to poke around. I'm not hiding anything. LOL!

Make yourself at home. Move things around to however you like.

I'm praying for you, Ariel. I believe God has something special in store for you during your time in Sanctuary.

Love, Gwyneth

Ariel set the note back on the counter. "I hope you're right, Gwyneth. I really hope you're right."

TOM FULLER LOOKED out his kitchen window, thankful they'd made it home from the ferry before the downpour. Lights were on at the Muldoon house. "Hey, Shauna."

"Yeah."

"Looks like Miss Gwyneth's friend got here while we were gone."

His eleven-year-old daughter came into the kitchen in a flash. That's how she did most things. She rushed. She raced. She flew. Now she hopped onto the counter with ease and looked out the window with him. "Let's take her some cookies. That's the friendly thing to do. Right, Dad?"

"It sure is, kiddo." He pushed kinky red curls away

from her face. "Go ahead and bake some."

Shauna dropped to the floor, and in no time at all, she had the oven preheating, she'd taken the roll of cookie dough from a shelf in the refrigerator and retrieved a knife from the utensil drawer. As she peeled back the plastic on the dough, she asked, "Do you know what her name is?" She began slicing, concentrating hard, her tongue peeking out the corner of her mouth.

"Hmm. Miss Gwyneth told me, but I forget what it was."

"That's not good."

"You're right. I should've paid more attention. I'll do better next time."

Shauna went to a cupboard beneath the counter and removed a large cookie sheet. She placed the twelve round slices of cookie dough on the pan, careful to have the same distance between each one of them. Watching his daughter, Tom reached for the oven mitts so he would be ready when the timer sounded, letting them know the oven had reached the desired temperature. He didn't have long to wait.

Half an hour later, with Tom holding an umbrella and Shauna carrying a plastic container holding almost a dozen warm sugar cookies, the two of them walked to the neighbor's front door. Shauna rang the bell. When no one answered, she rang it again. This time, Tom saw movement through the frosted glass. Then the door opened a couple of inches.

Tom smiled as he leaned to the right so the woman could see him better. "Hi. I'm Tom Fuller. This is my daughter, Shauna."

"We brought cookies to say welcome to the island." Shauna held up the container. "They're still warm and really good."

The door opened wider, and he got his first glimpse of Gwyneth's unnamed friend. She was slender and pretty with wavy brown hair falling around her shoulders. But it was her eyes that captured his attention. Not truly blue and not truly green, but somewhere in-between. Aquamarine, he thought. And amazing.

He cleared his throat and repeated, "I'm Tom Fuller."

"I'm Ariel Highbridge."

"Hey, you were on the ferry. Dad, she was on the ferry with us."

That was hard for him to believe. This time of year there weren't many passengers on the ferry. If he'd seen her, he would have remembered. Surely he would have.

"You're right. I was on the ferry." Ariel opened the door the rest of the way. "I'm sorry. Come in out of the rain. Please."

Tom closed the umbrella and leaned it next to the door on the stoop before stepping inside. Thankfully, Shauna didn't dash into the house, dripping water everywhere. When Gwyneth was here during the summers, his daughter treated this house like it was her second home, going in and out almost at will.

Shauna offered the container of cookies again. "There was a dozen, but I ate two."

Ariel laughed softly as she accepted the plastic box. "I love sugar cookies. Did you bake them yourself?"

"Yes." She glanced up. "Dad helped a little."

Ariel lifted her gaze. "Then I must thank you, too." She

smiled again.

It had been ages since Tom reacted to a woman's eyes or a woman's smile. In the first couple of years after his wife died, he'd spent most days in a haze of grief, just putting one foot in front of the other and trying to be both dad and mom to his daughter. But even in the last couple of years—as friends had begun to bug him about getting out there, dating, really living again—he'd failed to feel even a spark of interest in the women he met.

Until now.

"How come you're staying in Miss Gwyneth's house?" Shauna asked, ever the curious one.

If Ariel minded his daughter's bluntness, she didn't show it. "I wanted to get away for a while, and she thought I'd like to stay here for the winter."

"Where're you from?"

"Shauna," he warned softly.

"I live in Idaho. Do you know where that is?"

Shauna screwed up her face in thought, then answered, "Almost to the Pacific Ocean."

"You're right. It is almost to the ocean. Idaho comes just before Washington and Oregon."

Tom decided he'd better take his daughter home before she gave Ariel the complete third degree. Not that he wasn't interested in hearing Ariel's answers. He would like to know more about what she did in Idaho, where she lived, what brought her to Sanctuary Island for the winter, and plenty more. But now was not the time.

With a hand on Shauna's shoulder, he said, "We'll go now and let you settle in. We're right next door if you need anything. Don't hesitate to ask if you do."

"Thank you, Mr. Fuller."

"Tom. My name's Tom."

"Except when he's at school," Shauna interjected. "He's always Mr. Fuller there. Even *I've* gotta call him Mr. Fuller when we're at school." She ended with a roll of her eyes and a soft huff of air.

"Come on, you." He turned Shauna toward the door, and they went back out into the rain.

CHAPTER 2

Ariel was awakened the next morning by a familiar ringtone on her phone. Still sleepy, she grabbed it and pressed it to her ear. "This better be good, Gwyneth."

Her friend's laughter came through the speaker.

"I'm serious." Ariel lifted her head and looked for the clock. "What time is it?"

"Time you were up and getting ready for church."

"Are you my mother now?" She sat up, pushing a hank of hair back from her face with her free hand.

"No, but you need to meet people so your stay will be a good one."

"I came here to write. I do that alone with my laptop."

"You're there to refresh and renew yourself. *Then* you will write. Best place to refresh and renew is in church. You know that as well as I do."

"Nag. Nag. Nag." Now seated on the side of the bed, Ariel searched for her slippers with her toes.

"It's good for you. You need to do what's good for you."

"All right. All right. I've got to hang up now so I can shower and blow my hair dry."

Gwyneth laughed again.

"Wait. Where's the church?"

Her friend gave the directions to Sanctuary Bible Church, then Ariel ended the call and tossed the phone onto the bed.

A short while later, she stood in the shower beneath the spray of hot water, working shampoo into a lather. Now that she was fully awake, she was glad for her friend's call. It was important to gather together with other believers, and she might as well get to know the people she would worship beside for the coming months. Better today than waiting a week.

With her wet hair wrapped in a towel, she retrieved her phone from the bed and checked the weather. Cloudy and windy with morning temps in the forties, not counting the wind chill factor. The forecast determined her wardrobe—jeans, bulky sweater, and Uggs it would be.

Ariel left the house at twenty minutes to the hour, her Bible clutched inside her warm coat. It wasn't a long walk to the church. Only four blocks to the east. But it felt longer because of the gusty wind, and she was thankful when she stepped through the doors of the church and was met with stillness.

The stillness was short lived.

"Miss Highbridge!" Shauna Fuller hurried up to her. "We didn't know you'd be here."

Ariel raised her eyes and found Tom Fuller standing by the open sanctuary doors, beige-colored bulletins in one hand and a welcoming smile on his lips. It was a nice smile. She'd noticed that yesterday when he and Shauna delivered the fresh-baked cookies. A nice smile in a ruggedly handsome face.

Not that his looks mattered to her. Not in the least. Ariel had sworn off men. Her romantic life had been one disaster after another, and the most recent disaster undoubtedly played into the writer's block plaguing her.

Shauna took hold of one of Ariel's hands. "Come on. I'll show you around." The girl pulled her toward the sanctuary.

"Welcome," Tom said as she got closer. "We're glad you joined us." He held out a bulletin.

She took it. "Thanks."

"I'm gonna show her around."

Tom looked at his daughter. "Shouldn't you be in Sunday School? It'll start soon."

"I wanna stay with you today. And Miss Highbridge oughta have a friend to sit with. Shouldn't she?"

Ariel knew something about little girls who could wrap their dads around their little fingers. She'd been one of them. For an instant, she imagined her own father standing nearby, watching her and smiling, ready to say yes to anything she asked.

"All right." Tom met Ariel's gaze again. "If Ariel doesn't mind?"

"I don't mind."

And with that, Shauna tugged her into the sanctuary.

Within no time at all, Ariel had been introduced to Mr. Williams, owner of the Whimsical Pages Book Store; Mrs. Tony, who taught third and fourth grades at the school;

15

Mark and Phil Patrick, twin brothers who worked as bell-hops during the season at the Shore View Palace; and several other people whose names were forgotten in a blur of introductions. She was thankful when Shauna seemed satisfied and led the way into one of the wooden pews.

When the service began, Tom Fuller came to stand beside his daughter as the congregation sang a familiar hymn. Ariel was soon focused on the words of praise and found herself thanking God for Gwyneth's not-so-gentle urging that got her out of bed and into church.

Step one in renewing her creativity: Put God first in all things, and the rest would work itself out.

Tom knew how small towns worked, having lived in Sanctuary for most of his life. People would notice him sharing the pew with Ariel Highbridge, and there would be gossip. After all, he'd sat by himself in church for the last four years. By choice. People would notice the change.

It was all he could do not to groan in frustration at the thought of what people might say. He didn't want to be the subject of Sunday dinner conversations. Especially since there was no truth to whatever would be said. He barely knew the woman.

When the service ended—while Ariel talked to Grace Hawthorn, who'd been seated on her right—Tom steered Shauna toward the sanctuary exit, doing his best to avoid eye contact with his friends and neighbors. Not an easy task when his daughter wanted to talk to everyone she knew—and she knew everyone.

"Come on," he said in a low voice. "I want to leave now."

As they passed through the church doors, Shauna gave him a *What's wrong?* look. He ignored it and set a brisk pace as they followed the sidewalk toward home.

After the first block was behind them, he slowed a little. What *was* wrong with him? It was a fair question. Shauna had been polite to a visitor and made her feel welcome in church. That was all. Maybe the other people in church hadn't even noticed Ariel seated on the other side of Shauna. Maybe he was the only person in the sanctuary who'd been aware of her close proximity.

His pace slowed even more.

After Christina died, Tom had been determined to protect their daughter from any additional pain. He hadn't wanted someone coming into their lives who might leave and hurt Shauna with yet another loss in her life. And, if he were honest, he'd needed to protect himself as well. His and Shauna's hearts had been wounded enough by Christina's death. But maybe his friends and family were right. Maybe it was time to let his guard down. At least a little.

Heaven knew, he had been *very* aware of Ariel's close proximity this morning. So much so he'd barely heard a word of the sermon.

As they approached the house, Tom heard their dog barking. "Did you remember to feed Scruffy before we left for church?"

"I forgot. I'm sorry, Dad."

Before Tom could say more, Shauna took off running. "Clean water, too," he called after her. She didn't even break her stride as she waved an arm in acknowledgment.

He grinned and said a silent thanks to God. She was a good kid. She was a happy kid. Despite the mistakes he'd made as a single parent—and he'd made more than a few —he hadn't ruined Shauna's childhood. Not yet anyway.

Which brought his thoughts back to Ariel Highbridge. Could it hurt to get to know her? They would be living next door to each other until spring, and Gwyneth had asked him to look out for her good friend.

It hadn't been very neighborly to leave church without even saying goodbye. He winced. But maybe she hadn't noticed. Grace would have been making Ariel feel more than welcome. No, Ariel probably hadn't even noticed he and Shauna had slipped away so fast. At least, he hoped not.

Upon entering the house, he heard the rapid tapping of toenails on the linoleum floor, and he could picture Scruffy dancing all around his daughter. He'd seen it often enough.

"Get outta the way, Scruffy."

The sound of kibble landing in a metal bowl met him as he walked into the kitchen.

"He's starved, Dad. Sorry I forgot."

"He may be hungry, but he's anything but starved." Tom leaned on the doorjamb of the laundry room and observed the action.

The dog in question was a Heinz-Fifty-Seven mutt Shauna had selected at an animal shelter in Havensport. Scruffy had been named for the way he looked. The vet said the little dog should weigh no more than twenty pounds, but at his last annual, he'd weighed in at twenty-five. That hadn't sounded too bad to Tom until he realized how fat he would be if he went up an extra fourth of his current weight. No, Scruffy definitely wasn't starving.

While the dog scarfed down his kibble, Shauna took another bowl to the laundry room sink and filled it to the brim. Then she carefully measured the water additive—meant to keep Scruffy's teeth clean and his breath smelling better—and poured it into the bowl.

Pushing off the doorjamb, Tom asked, "Now what about us? What are you hungry for?"

"Hot dogs and mac and cheese."

"We had that Wednesday."

"Spaghetti?"

He opened the fridge and looked inside. "No hamburger defrosted and neither is the sauce. How about grilled cheese sandwiches and tomato soup."

"Sure. Can I make the sandwiches?"

"You bet. Wash your hands good before you start."

"Dad." Shauna drew out the name as if it were six syllables long. "I always do."

Tom laughed. He loved Sundays at home with his daughter after church. They never ceased to remind him that God is good no matter the circumstances of life.

CHAPTER 3

T om always thought there was something abnormal about a classroom after the kids went home. Sure, it was quiet so he could get tasks done. But if he were honest, he missed the sound of kids breathing, the sniffing of noses, the shuffle of feet on the floor, the tapping of fingers on desktops, the scratch of pencils on paper.

Tom had been the combined fifth and sixth grade teacher for the Sanctuary Island School District for the past twelve years. The number of students in his classroom varied from year to year, but he averaged about eleven or twelve. His smallest class size had been the year with three fifth graders and four sixth graders. This year he had six fifth graders and nine sixth graders, an unusually large class. One of those sixth graders was his daughter, and this was his second year to be Shauna's teacher. He found that both a challenge and a blessing. Don't play favorites but don't be too tough either. Find a balance between being a teacher and being Dad. It could be tricky.

The squeak of shoes coming from the hallway told him Shauna had returned. Meg Harlowe, Sanctuary's beloved piano teacher, lived across the street from the school. If kids on the island wanted to learn to play the piano, Meg was usually the one who taught them. Thus, every Monday, right after school let out, Shauna crossed West Fifth Street to take another lesson from the venerable pianist. This was Shauna's second year of lessons, and Tom was proud of her for sticking with it.

His daughter appeared in the classroom doorway. "You ready, Dad?"

"I'm ready, Peanut." He started to gather up papers when his phone notified him he had a text. He slipped it from his shirt pocket.

> GWYNETH MULDOON:
>
> Just learned there's to be a writing contest as part of Christmas festival. You should ask Ariel for help. Who better than a novelist?

A novelist? Had Gwyneth told him Ariel was a writer? He didn't think so. All the same, it would be great if she would talk to his class. Something to excite them about participating in the writing contest.

> TOM FULLER:
>
> Thanks for the tip.

Tom slid the phone into his pocket again.

The walk home never took long, no matter the weather, as the Fuller house was only two blocks from the school.

"I got three gold stars on the music I played today. Mrs. Harlowe says I'll get a new lesson book after Christmas. Maybe next year I'll be ready to play for the Christmas Eve service at church. You think I will?"

"Maybe. Mrs. Harlowe would know better than me. I think everything you play sounds great."

"Dad." There was that six syllable name again.

"Well, it's true. But there's something else I want to know. About the stories you like to write."

"What'd'ya mean?"

"You're always writing stories in your journals. I'm wondering if you'll enter any of them in the festival contest?"

"I haven't made up any Christmas stories."

Tom placed his hand on her shoulder as they prepared to cross the street. "You've got time. The entries don't have to be turned in for another month."

"I guess I could. I don't know. They're kinda silly, the stuff I write."

"You know what? Our new neighbor is a writer. Miss Gwyneth said she writes novels."

Shauna looked at him with wide eyes. "Really? You mean, like books?"

"Like books."

"Cool."

The subject of their conversation stepped out through her front doorway just as Tom and Shauna reached the curb.

"Hi, Miss Highbridge." Shauna ran ahead of him. "Dad says you're a writer. Are you?"

Ariel hesitated, then answered, "Yes, I am."

"Cool. I like to write."

"That's great." Ariel's gaze shifted to Tom as he neared the walk to her house. "I was hoping to talk to you, Mr. Fuller. Your dog dug under the fence and is sitting on my back porch." A frown furrowed her brow. "He's been whining. For hours."

"Scruffy's at your house?" Shauna came toward Ariel. "I'll get him."

Ariel didn't have time to react before Shauna shot past her.

"Sorry," Tom said. "Gwyneth has an open door policy when it comes to Shauna."

"So I see." Ariel's smile replaced her less-than-pleased expression. "You'd better come inside too."

"Thanks."

She turned, and he followed behind. By the time they reached the living room, Shauna was there, holding Scruffy in her arms.

"He's kinda dirty, Dad."

An understatement if Tom ever heard one. There was more dried mud than dog in his daughter's arms. "You take him home and clean him up. I'll have Miss Highbridge show me where Scruffy got through the fence."

Shauna was out of the house almost as fast as she'd entered it.

"Follow me," Ariel said. "I wasn't sure what to do to fix it or I would have taken him back to your place myself."

"You shouldn't have to fix it. He's our dog. I'll take care of it."

They went out to the porch and down the back steps.

"I was sitting at the desk, trying to write, when I saw him squeeze under the fence. Right there." She pointed.

No wonder Scruffy was covered in chunks of dried mud. He'd made quite a hole on both sides of the fence, but he would have had to squeeze through, all the same.

"Determined, wasn't he?" Tom faced Ariel. "He's done some digging in our yard, but never anything like this. I'm sorry he bothered you."

"Don't worry about it." Her sigh said more than words. "The writing wasn't going well anyway."

"Sorry to hear that."

She released a humorless laugh. "At least this time I could blame it on the dog." With that, she turned and walked toward the house.

Tom followed, wondering about her comment and—strangely—wishing there was something he could do to help.

ARIEL STOOD near the desk overlooking the backyard. From there she could see Tom on the other side of the fence, filling the hole. But what would he do to keep the dog from digging under it again?

"Not my problem."

No, her problem had to do with a book deadline and the words she couldn't seem to put on the page. Her well was dry, and she hadn't a clue how to refill it.

Her writer friends had been quick to make suggestions. Try writing something completely different.

Get a hobby. Journal about herself, her life, the story. Take long walks. Redecorate a room. Take a trip. The list went on and on. She'd tried many of them, including moving herself to a remote island for the winter.

Maybe that had been a bit desperate.

She sighed as she sat on the chair at the desk.

It didn't help that she was a romance writer who had failed utterly in the real-life romance department. After a messy breakup with Zach Miller at the start of last summer, she'd sworn off men. All they did was lie to her, misuse her, break her heart. Romance didn't exist these days. Not the type of romance she wanted anyway.

So how was she supposed to write about love?

It should make things easier that she set her stories in Regency England. That was definitely a more romantic era. It should help, but it didn't.

A tone alerted her to a FaceTime call. An instant after accepting it, her mom appeared on the screen.

"Hi, honey."

"Hi, Mom."

"You got to the island all safe and sound then."

She was tempted to remind her mom that she wasn't twelve. Instead, she answered, "I got here without any problems. The flights were mostly smooth, and I tried to sleep most of the way. The ferry ride was choppy but I loved it. I stood outside and imagined I was a pirate on a ship at sea, standing at the helm."

Her mom laughed. "You and that crazy imagination. No wonder God made you a writer. Did you go to church yesterday? Gwyneth seems to really love the people there."

"Yes, I went to church. And I met Gwyneth's neighbors and lots of her friends. I'm certain I'll get lots of work done here, too. It's just what I need." She wasn't certain of any such thing, but she hoped it would make her mom worry less about her.

The sound of pounding intruded on her thoughts, and she looked out the window again. She couldn't see Tom now, but the noise said he was out there. What on earth was he doing?

"Mom, the neighbor's dog dug under the fence, and he's trying to fix it so it won't happen again. I think I need to go see what he's doing."

"All right, honey. Let's talk again soon."

"We will. Give my love to Wes."

"I'll do it. Have a good evening."

"Love you."

"Love you back."

After tapping to end the video call, she stood and retrieved her coat from the tree in the entry hall, then stepped onto the back porch. Nightfall was no more than an hour away, and the temperature had dropped even lower than when she'd shown Tom where Scruffy dug under the fence. She crossed her arms over her chest, hugging her coat tight against her.

"How's it going?" she called.

The top of Tom's head and his eyes came into view. "Okay."

"I heard pounding."

"I'm driving metal stakes into the ground."

"Will that be enough?"

"No. This is temporary. We've got a lot of fence, and I don't have many stakes." He disappeared from view, and the slow pounding began again.

Ariel spied a plastic stool—three steps tall—beside the shed and went to get it. After placing it next to the fence, she stood on it, looking down on Tom on the opposite side. "You do have a lot of fence," she said. "So what will you do to keep him from digging in a different spot?"

He straightened. Then he grinned, as if pleased to see her.

A fluttery sensation started in her stomach.

"I looked online for what could stop a dog from digging under a fence. I found a metal guard you drive into the ground along the fence, kind of like what I'm doing now, only more effective. Each panel is over a foot wide. You drive a panel into the ground about six to ten inches deep or more, leaving at least four inches above ground." He turned, apparently taking in the entire fence line, before he met her gaze again. "I could get my order by Friday. Saturday at the latest. Scruffy can stay in the house during the day until the weekend. I'll come home to let him out at lunchtime, and Saturday I'll get the guards hammered into the ground. He won't be in your yard whining at the door again."

Feeling a sting of guilt, she said, "It wasn't that bad."

Tom laughed. "Yes, it was. I've had to listen to him whine a time or two myself. I know how irritating it can be."

Okay, it *had* been an annoying sound. But she couldn't blame her inability to write on the dog. "When those metal guards arrive, let me know. I'll help you get them in the ground."

Surprise filled his dark brown eyes, but she didn't give him a chance to say anything before she stepped off the stool, dropping out of view. "Good night, Tom." She hurried to the house.

CHAPTER 4

The Island Market was even smaller than Ariel expected. It was quickly apparent why Gwyneth said year-round residents did most of their shopping on the mainland. Still, Ariel had never found pleasure in cooking for one and was perfectly willing to open a can or a box when she was ready to eat. She could survive on the basics. Peanut butter, jam, and crackers served in a pinch.

With Gwyneth's wheeled cart filled with bags of canned soup, chili, and green beans, along with a small block of cheese, some apples, a loaf of bread, a box of cereal, and a quart of skim milk, Ariel started back toward the house, then decided to take a walk through town instead. Even if most shops weren't open in the off-season, she could still take in the charm of the place and imagine what it would be like in the summer when thousands of day tourists, long-term guests, and summer residents flooded the island.

And anything was preferable to staring at a blank laptop screen.

She'd walked about four blocks when she smelled something delicious. Cookies maybe? Her mouth watered, and her footsteps quickened in response. The town was quiet on a Wednesday morning—it was probably quiet most days of the week in the off-season—but when she turned the corner and saw several people standing outside a shop with a pink and blue awning, she knew her nose hadn't steered her wrong. She hurried on.

Two women—one appeared to be in her twenties, the other in her late forties or early fifties—smiled at Ariel as she approached.

"Morning," the older one said.

"Good morning," Ariel returned as she glanced at the sign in the window. *Cathy's Cupcakes*, it read. Ah, one of the places Gwyneth had mentioned in her note. She got in line.

"Are you new to the island?" the younger woman asked.

"Yes. I arrived on Saturday."

"Welcome to Sanctuary. I'm Abigail, and this is my mom, Kelly."

"Hi. I'm Ariel." She nodded at them both.

Abigail glanced toward the shop window. "Have you been here before?"

"No."

"Well, you've found one of our favorite places on the island. Cathy's cupcakes are delish. My favorite's the Boston creme pie. Mom loves the carrot cake. My dad's partial to the red velvet."

As a customer left the shop, the open door let out even more of the delicious aromas. Ariel's anticipation increased.

"Get an extra one or two," Abigail added. "Cathy's is only open on Wednesdays from eleven until two and Saturdays from eleven until four."

"Thanks for the tip."

The small bakery, when Ariel finally made it through the corner doorway, had only enough room for three or four customers on the front side of the display case. There was no seating. The shop was meant for buying and taking home.

Waiting her turn, she read the menu. There were thirteen different cupcake options. And pup-cakes, a treat for four-legged family members. Ariel thought of Scruffy.

The girl behind the counter wore a bored expression, along with a nose ring and bubblegum pink hair worn short and spiky. "Can I help you?" She sounded as bored as she looked.

"Yes, please. I'd like the four-pack of pup-cakes, plus a Boston Creme and a Lemon Drop. Oh, and one of the Buttercremes, too." She thought of Tom and Shauna. How could she take over the dog treats and not take something for the humans? "You know what. Make it two of each of those cupcake flavors."

"Sure." The girl rang up her order.

The total due was slightly shocking, but Ariel managed not to flinch. She removed her credit card from the back of her phone case and was ready for the girl when she returned with the box of cupcakes and the small sack holding the dog treats.

In warmer weather, Ariel might have walked to the town square and sat in the gazebo to eat one of the cupcakes. But the chilly breeze made her hasten on home. She would explore more of the town with its charming historic houses and cobblestone streets another time.

~

THANKFUL IT WASN'T RAINING, Tom headed for home as soon as his class released for lunch. Even more thankful it wasn't snowing, although his weather app showed the possibility before the next ten days were over.

When Tom stuck his key in the lock, Scruffy barked and jumped against the door. Translation: *Hurry up out there. I've gotta go.*

"Hey, boy." He eased the door open. "Give me a second." He stepped inside and closed the door behind him. "Ready to go out?"

Scruffy ran a couple of circles around him.

"Come on." Tom walked into the laundry room and opened the back door. "There you go."

Scruffy zoomed past him.

Tom followed the dog outside. "Do your business. And no digging."

Scruffy was quick to obey the first command. Whether or not the dog would have foregone digging, Tom wouldn't know because the doorbell rang, and that sound was more effective than the sound of kibble pouring into a bowl. Scruffy raced into the house, barking all the way to the front door, then he raced back to Tom, circled him, and ran to the door again.

"Crazy dog. Get back. Get back." With his foot, he brushed Scruffy away from the door so he could open it.

On the stoop stood Ariel Highbridge, her puffy winter coat zipped up to her chin. She held a covered plate and a small sack in her hands. "I come bearing gifts."

Why gifts? He opened the door wide. "Come in out of the cold."

"Thanks." She walked into the house and continued on into the kitchen. "I explored a little in town this morning and discovered Cathy's Cupcakes."

Tom chuckled. "The ruination of many a waistline."

"That's what I'm afraid of." She set the plate and brown lunch sack on the counter, then opened the sack and pulled out a treat both Tom and Scruffy recognized. "I brought a peace offering for your little friend."

Scruffy stood on his back legs and danced in a circle.

Ariel laughed. It was a light, airy sound that swirled around Tom like a magical vapor, lifting his mood. And maybe, for a second, it lifted him off the floor. At least it felt that way.

"Here you go, Scruffy." Ariel rewarded the dog.

Had Scruffy even tasted the treat before he swallowed? Tom doubted it. A couple of chews and the pup-cake was gone. Scruffy sniffed around the floor, hoping for dropped crumbs. Then he turned pleading eyes on Ariel, his new best friend.

"The way to Scruffy's heart is definitely through his stomach," Tom said. "Thus the extra weight he's packing."

"I made him stay outside in the cold the other day, just because he was covered in mud. Then I blamed his whining for why I couldn't get any writing done. I needed to tell him I'm sorry." She knelt beside Scruffy and fed him another pup-cake.

What a softie she was. And Tom adored her for it. "I'm betting you're a dog person," he said.

She nodded as she rose. "Her name was Ditto. I got her as a puppy when I was twelve, and we did everything together, except when I went to college. Then my parents kept her. Ditto lived to be fifteen. I was heartbroken when she died."

"It's tough to lose them. That's the biggest downside to dogs. They just don't live long enough."

Ariel nodded again before looking away.

Had he seen tears in her eyes?

"I should let you be," she said.

"I was going to make myself a sandwich. Chicken salad. Why not stay and eat with me? I've got about half an hour before I have to be back at the school."

She looked like she was going to refuse but surprised him by saying, "Thank you. I'd like that."

"Have a seat." He motioned to the table. "This won't take me long."

Tom took a container of chicken salad from the fridge and four slices of honey wheat bread from the plastic bread bag. The finished sandwiches were on the table in short order. A bag of chips and two glasses of water quickly followed.

As he sat opposite Ariel, he asked, "Mind if I give thanks?"

"No. I'd like that."

He bowed his head, took a slow breath to center his thoughts, then prayed. "For food in a world where many walk in hunger; for faith in a world where many walk in fear; for friends in a world where many walk alone, we give You thanks, O Lord. Amen." He raised his eyes and found her watching him with a soft expression.

"That was a beautiful blessing," she said.

"It's an old Jesuit prayer. I stumbled across it years ago, and it became my favorite words to pray over a meal."

"I can see why. Would you write it down for me?"

"Sure."

She lifted the sandwich from her plate and took a bite. "Mmm. That's good. Did you make the chicken salad yourself?"

"I did."

"Lots of the guys I've known would struggle to make their own bologna sandwich."

Tom laughed softly. "I got a crash course in cooking and baking a few years back. With lots of help from some of the women at church." His smile faded at the memory. "After my wife died, I had to learn how to feed Shauna more than hot dogs and mac and cheese. Although those are still among her favorites."

"I . . . I'm sorry about your wife. How long ago was it?"

"Four years, the end of last August. It was sudden. An infection led to sepsis, and she was gone."

"I'm sorry," Ariel repeated. "I lost my dad when I was twenty. It was sudden too. A heart attack. I still miss him."

"I expected grief to run on some sort of time clock. You know. Like each stage of grief should take exactly a month and then be done. I found out it's a lot more chaotic than that. But then it's different for everybody."

"And you had a little girl to take care of, and she was grieving too."

Her understanding warmed his heart. "Yeah. But having Shauna to care for was a blessing. I had to keep going for her. Be strong for her."

"Do you have any other family?"

"None on the island. Christina . . . that was my wife . . . her parents live on the mainland. They came over and stayed for several weeks after Christina died. We see them quite a bit. My parents moved to Arizona before Shauna was born, but they come every summer for a nice long visit, and Shauna and I fly down to see them every year. It's my church family who were the constant, day-to-day source of help I needed when I was at my lowest. I thank God for them often."

He picked up his sandwich, signaling an end to that particular topic of conversation. Ariel took the cue from him and returned her attention to her own sandwich. The silence that followed wasn't uncomfortable, which surprised Tom. In fact it felt as comfortable as a well-worn, often-washed T-shirt. When he brought up a new topic after a short while, it wasn't to end the silence but because he was curious.

"Tell me about your writing. Gwyneth told me you're a novelist."

"Yes." Her expression remained neutral.

"What is it you write?"

"Regency romances for the Christian market."

How should he reply? He knew nothing about that genre.

"They're love stories set during the British Regency,"

she added. "Mostly during the years of 1811 to 1820. Think Jane Austen. Not that my writing is anything as wonderful as hers. *Pride and Prejudice* is probably my favorite book of all time."

"The research must be interesting."

"It is." She glanced away, staring off into space. "Although I'm not particularly inspired by it lately."

He was tempted to press for more information but decided to go a different direction. "Would you be at all interested in talking to my students?"

She met his gaze again. "Me?"

"Sure. Kids love it when we have guest speakers telling them about their jobs. Especially when they have such an interesting one. I've got some students who are good writers. Shauna among them. They're young, of course, but they'll love being able to ask you questions." He stood, picked up both of their plates, and carried them to the sink. "They're having a writing contest as part of the Christmas festival this year. You could encourage the kids to enter it. That would be a real bonus."

And maybe he would see more of Ariel because of it. Which he was starting to think would be another bonus.

CHAPTER 5

Friday, November 7, 2024, 9:07 AM

Hi, Ariel.

How's Michigan? Do you like staying on an island? We miss you around here. Hope the getaway does you good.

It's gorgeous here in Boise. It's going to be sixty degrees today. The pretty colors are mostly over, and there are lots of leaves on the ground. Jason has been blowing leaves and stuffing them in leaf bags. He keeps threatening to cut down the trees in our yard.

I don't know if I should tell you this or not, but I didn't want you to hear it any other way. Zach is getting married next month to Cynthia Murphy. A Christmas Eve wedding. They had the nerve to send me an invitation.

I know your breakup with Zach happened months ago, and you are over him. But if you need to talk, please call me. Vent all you want. I'm always willing to listen.

I hope you're writing again.

Love you,

Danni

---

riel closed the top of her laptop and stared out the window, the words from her friend's email replaying in her mind.

Zach's getting married.

She waited to feel pain. None came.

Zach Miller, her boyfriend of almost two years, was movie star handsome with black hair, hazel eyes, olive skin, and chiseled features. He was charming, adventurous, and exciting. She'd fallen for him. Hard. He'd gone to church with her a Sunday or two a month, and he'd even stopped pressuring her about sex before marriage. He'd said the right things at the right time. She'd thought he was the real deal. But over time, she'd begun to see a few flaws. What she hadn't seen was the deception and how easy it was for him to lie to her. When she'd discovered he'd been sleeping with Cynthia Murphy—all of nineteen years old, looking like a twenty-pound-underweight swimsuit model—Ariel had felt hurt and betrayed. But any heartbreak she'd experienced because of Zach was gone by this time. Completely forgotten.

What she felt now was frustration. Not about her love life, which didn't exist—well, maybe a little of her frustration was about the lack of a love life—but with her life as a writer. She'd struggled to come up with a new story idea for months. Yes, the breakup had played a part in those struggles. It was difficult to write a romantic story when she'd stopped believing she would experience romance for herself. But now that she was over the hurt of Zach's betrayal, shouldn't she also be over this blasted writer's block, too?

It didn't help matters that, at the end of last July, Ariel's editor, Bridget Bloom, had given birth to her first baby and immediately decided to stay home to be a full-time mom. Ariel had been devastated by the news. She'd never worked with any editor except Bridget. It had been Bridget who bought Ariel's first book and who'd worked on the nine novels that followed. What if Ariel couldn't work as well with the new editor she'd been assigned? Not that it would matter unless she started writing again. She had zip, nada, nothing written on her next book. It wasn't due until the end of May, which was more than enough time to write one of her books under normal circumstances. But it wouldn't be enough time if she didn't get off her behind soon.

What was wrong with her? Ever since the idea for what had become her first book popped into her head, she'd never lacked for ideas, enthusiasm, or a willingness to sit down at her computer and type and type and type. She loved the act of writing. She loved having written. She loved digging through research books. She loved carefully crafting her characters, characters who became real people in her mind. Sometimes they even whispered to her in her dreams.

But no character had whispered to her for months.

She had no story and therefore no characters. She felt abandoned, alone, rejected.

"Maybe they're gone for good."

She groaned. She wasn't ready to admit defeat. She didn't want to stop being a writer.

Leave your laptop, one piece of advice read, *and go do something fun.*

Give it to God, was her mom's bit of wisdom.

Ariel rose from the desk chair, put on her coat, and headed out into the cold morning. The skies were gray again and rain was promised by the afternoon. Rather fitting for her mood.

If she couldn't write, she was no longer a writer. No wonder she'd wanted to refuse when Tom Fuller asked her to talk to his class. How could she stand in front of a bunch of ten- and eleven-year-olds and say how great it was to be a writer? They would shout back at her, "Fraud!"

Her walk took her past the school and into the center of town. On a Saturday, she would have headed for Cathy's Cupcakes. Nothing like a sugar-high to beat back the blues. Right? But today was Friday. She wouldn't find solace in frosted cakes today.

Her hopes rose again when she saw the sign for the bookstore. She hurried to the end of the block and went inside. She was met with warm air and the lovely smell of books. Behind the counter on her right, a man offered a friendly smile. She recognized him from church. Mr. Williams, Shauna had called him.

"Welcome to Whimsical Pages," he said. Tall and stocky with pale reddish hair, she guessed him to be in his fifties. He had a nice face, and something about him told her he actually knew books.

"Thank you."

"I'm Guy Williams."

"I'm Ariel. We met in church."

"Oh, that's right. You're Shauna's friend."

Ariel laughed softly. "Yes."

"May I help you find something?"

"Just browsing."

"All right. Enjoy. Call for me if you need anything."

With a nod, she moved on.

Shelves lined the walls on the sides and back, reaching almost to the ceiling. Freestanding shelves filled the rest of the store, and the aisles between them were narrow, giving a customer only enough room to bend down to search a bottom shelf without hitting their backside against the opposite bookshelf. The latest bestsellers and new releases held places of prominence at the front of the store. Deep in the back, there were used books. Like old friends, they beckoned to her.

Fiction filled the shelves to her right. On the other side of a door, non-fiction filled another large section. She moved to the non-fiction books. She'd found many a research gem in the backs of used bookstores and at library sales. Books she hadn't known she would need but had proven indispensable. Writers who were older than Ariel often told her how much the internet and ebooks had changed the way authors did research. But there was something wonderful about holding an old hardcover in her hands.

When it came to old books, if Ariel ever had unlimited

funds, she would buy a first edition of *Pride and Prejudice*. About a hundred and seventy-five thousand dollars, the last time she'd checked.

"I won't hold my breath," she whispered as she ran her fingers along the spines of the books at eye level.

She lost track of time as she browsed, sometimes pulling a book off a shelf and turning pages. She didn't find a book that demanded purchase, but she was reminded of how much she loved to read and of how much, in turn, she loved to write books for people who loved to read.

A very good thing to remember.

TOM STOOD inside the school exit doors, watching the students scatter in different directions. Today had been a half-day of school, and everyone seemed even more eager than usual to get away from school. Some had plans to go to Havensport for the weekend with their parents and siblings. He knew because he'd heard them talking about it.

While that wasn't true for Tom and Shauna—he had a backyard fence to make secure tomorrow—he had promised to take his daughter to Whimsical Pages before they went home. She'd pleaded for a new journal to use when writing her story for the festival, and he'd given in.

Once they left the school grounds, Shauna skipped ahead of him on the sidewalk. "Come on, Dad. Hurry up."

"It isn't a race."

"Daddy!"

He liked it when she slipped up and called him Daddy. That's what she used to call him all the time, right up until the start of this school year. Then, out of the blue, he'd become Dad.

Don't grow up too fast, kiddo. I'm not ready for it, even if you are.

Shauna ran back and took him by the hand in an attempt to hurry him along.

He laughed. "All right. All right."

The bookstore was located at the corner of West Third and Main. The owner, Guy Williams, stocked a great combination of bestsellers and lesser known works. There were shelves of both commercial and literary fiction. There were shelves of biographies and histories. There was a great children's section and a nice collection for young adult readers as well. While Tom loved to read for pleasure, he'd spent the past few years reading books about cooking, child rearing, and home repair, and he'd purchased quite a few of them at Whimsical Pages.

As soon as they entered the bookstore, Shauna headed for the display of journals.

From behind the counter, Guy said, "Don't see you in here most weekdays."

"Half day of school."

"Ah. May I help you find something?"

"Shauna knows what she wants. Maybe I'll just—" The rest of his words were interrupted when he saw Ariel walking toward him down the center aisle, holding several books against her chest.

"Miss Highbridge!" Shauna had seen her too, and his daughter moved quickly toward their neighbor. "Dad's getting me a new journal to write my story in. The one for the festival contest."

Ariel smiled. "That's nice. I love new journals."

"But I can't decide between the red one or the yellow one." Shauna held up a journal in each hand. "Yellow's my favorite color, but the story's for Christmas so maybe it should be in a red one."

Ariel leaned down, putting her head closer to Shauna's. "Which color will inspire you more?"

Shauna scrunched her face in thought. The expression always made Tom want to laugh.

Guy said, "I heard about the writing contest. That's a great addition to the festival."

"Miss Highbridge is a writer," Shauna told Guy, excitement in her voice. Then her eyes widened. "Do you have any of her books, Mr. Williams? I haven't seen any of her books. You got some?"

"Well, I don't know, Shauna." Guy looked at Ariel. "May I ask what name you write under and what sort of books you write?"

Before Ariel could answer, Shauna said, "Ariel Highbridge. She writes novels."

With a blush coloring her cheeks, Ariel looked more than a little uncomfortable. "My latest book is *Remembering the Duke*. It's a Regency romance." She named the publisher and the release date.

"Let me have a look." Guy disappeared down an aisle, and Shauna followed right behind him.

Ariel gave a little shrug of her shoulders as she met Tom's gaze. "I'll be surprised if he has a copy. That book came out in June."

"Dad!" Shauna reappeared, the two journals still clutched in one hand, a novel in another. "Look! He had one. Can I get it? Please!"

He felt trapped. Ariel had told him she wrote for the Christian market, but her stories were written for adults, not eleven-year-olds. Was it safe to let Shauna read one? On the other hand, he didn't want to offend Ariel by telling Shauna no.

"Shauna," Ariel said, leaning down to eye-level a second time, "have you read *Little Women?*"

His daughter's eyes lit up. "Yes. I *love* that book."

"Me, too. Jo is one of my favorite characters. What are some other favorite books of yours?"

"Dad read *Where the Red Fern Grows* with me. We both cried, but I liked it."

Ariel glanced up and smiled. "Both of you cried?"

"Both of us," Tom answered.

Ariel straightened. "Shauna, my books are love stories. They focus on the romance between a man and a woman. They're very different from those two novels."

"I know. But romance is nice."

"Is it?" Humor laced Ariel's question.

"Sure."

Ariel turned her eyes on Tom. "My novels would be rated PG, I think. I don't believe there is anything in *Remembering the Duke* that would be objectionable. But I'll understand if you think she should wait a year or two before she reads it."

She'd gracefully let him off the hook. But his own curiosity had been raised.

He looked at his daughter. "We can buy it, but I'll read

it first. Then, if I think it's okay for you, you can read it too."

"Okay, Dad. But you gotta read it fast. Deal?"

He laughed. "I'll do my best. Now decide which of those journals you want. We need to get home and let Scruffy out."

Shauna handed him the novel, then returned to the shelf where the journals were.

"Speaking of Scruffy," Ariel said, "will those fence guards arrive tomorrow?"

"Actually, I got a text. They'll be delivered today. May even be at my door already."

"What time tomorrow shall I come over to help with the installation? Or would this afternoon be better?"

"You don't have to help, you know. Our dog, our problem."

Her answering smile made him feel slightly breathless. Would that happen to the hero in her romance novel? Maybe. But it hadn't happened to him in so long the memory of it didn't seem real.

"Let's make it tomorrow," he answered at last. "Say eleven?"

"Eleven it is."

CHAPTER 6

On Saturday morning, Tom opened the boxes that contained the dig guards and placed the metal wire panels on the ground all along the fence. Scruffy wouldn't have a prayer of digging under any section of fence, and the pavers underneath the gate already protected that escape route.

After Tom finished the initial preparation, including putting three hammers on the back porch table, he returned inside and sat in his recliner. Next to his chair rested *Remembering the Duke* on a small round table. He'd read the first couple of chapters last night. He'd never imagined himself reading a romance novel. His tastes ran more towards military fiction with settings like ancient Rome or World War Two. Good old action-adventure stories. But the characters in Ariel's book had managed to capture his imagination. He already wanted to know what would happen to them.

He was reaching for the book when the doorbell rang.

"I'll get it!" Shauna called.

He heard his daughter and Scruffy run to the front door.

"Hi, Miss Highbridge. Come on in. Dad, she's here."

Tom stood and moved toward the entrance to the living room in time to see Ariel give Scruffy a friendly pat on the back.

When she straightened, she saw him and smiled. "Your workforce has arrived, Mr. Fuller."

Tom wondered if there was a boyfriend back in Idaho. From what he understood, Ariel had come to Sanctuary Island to work on her book. But that didn't mean she didn't have a love interest back home. Look at her. She was adorable, her thick long hair in a ponytail, her ears covered in fluffy muffs. Not to mention that she was charming and great with both his daughter and their dog. There must be a boyfriend somewhere. And even if there wasn't, he needed to be careful. Hers was a temporary stay.

Caution would be a good thing.

He took a quick breath, offered a smile, and reached for his coat and work gloves. "Let's get started then. Shauna, you need a hat and gloves too."

The instructions for the guards were simple. Drive each panel into the ground with a hammer, and if needed, they could be snapped together. That part didn't seem necessary, given how they were being used.

"Ground's frozen not very far down. We'll pound the panels as far as we can. If we can manage to go at least six inches deep, that ought to be good enough to keep Scruffy from repeating his last escapade. When the weather warms up, I can force them deeper if I need to."

The three of them tromped outside in the late morning chill. Their breaths formed little clouds in front of their mouths before dissipating. Scruffy ran circles around them, bouncing in excitement. After all, how often did he have three humans to play with?

Tom began in the northeast corner of the yard, driving a panel into the ground as deep as it would go. Ariel and Shauna observed him.

"Think you can do this?" he asked his daughter.

"Sure."

"Then you do the next one. I don't want you smashing a finger with the hammer, so I'll watch and see how you do."

"Okay." She lifted the panel off the ground, set it close to the one Tom had worked on, and pushed down on it with both hands. Once steady, she picked up the hammer and pounded it the same way he'd done.

"Perfect, kiddo. You don't need any more help from me." He turned and pointed at the southwest corner of the yard. "Why don't you start there, and I'll finish up here."

"Sure." Off Shauna ran.

"I can see why you became a teacher," Ariel said when Shauna was out of earshot. "You're really good with her."

"It's a little different, being a dad and being a teacher. But yeah. I like kids. And ten and eleven are good ages. Old enough to have rational conversations with them, and not yet crazy like they can be as teenagers." He glanced across the yard where Shauna had set to work with her hammer. "I'm hoping I won't totally blow it when she becomes a teen."

"You won't blow it."

"From your mouth to God's ears." He returned his gaze to Ariel, offering a wry smile. "That's what my grandmother always said."

"Shauna adores you. You'll both be fine."

"Maybe. But I wish her mom was here to help guide her as she grows into a young woman."

Ariel glanced down, then met his gaze again. "You must miss your wife terribly."

"I miss her. But it isn't as painful as it used to be." He bent to retrieve another panel, effectively putting an end to the conversation.

ARIEL'S STRETCH of the fence was nearly completed when her cell phone buzzed in the back pocket of her jeans. She reached to retrieve it. Her agent's name, Steven Kipping, and his photograph were on the screen.

She pressed the Accept button. "Hi, Steven."

"Good afternoon, Ariel."

His serious tone caused nerves to erupt in her belly. Was he about to ask how the book was going? She couldn't lie to him, but she didn't want to admit all she had was a document with a blank page. Not even a working title.

"Sorry to disturb on a Saturday, but I have news to pass on to you. News I felt couldn't wait until Monday."

That didn't sound like this was a call about her manuscript or its due date.

"Ariel, I'm closing my agency."

She sucked in a breath. "What? Why?"

"I won't bore you with details, but I've been appointed to a seat in my state legislature. Serving in government is something I have thought about for a long while, and I couldn't turn down this chance to get my foot in the door. While I could continue representing clients, I don't feel that would be fair, as I wouldn't always be available when needs require."

"I . . . I don't know what to say. I'm happy for you, of course. It's something you really want to do. But it's . . . it's such a shock."

"Don't worry about representation. I won't drop you like a hot potato." He chuckled. "I'm in talks with agents at a couple of other agencies. I'll find you the right fit. I promise."

"I appreciate that," she answered softly.

"I won't keep you any longer. I have more calls to make. Be assured, I'll be in touch as soon as I have any news for you."

"Thanks, Steven."

She stared at her phone long after ending the call. First her editor and now her agent. Both of them had abandoned her at the very worst time in her short-lived career. Perhaps abandoned might be too strong of a word, but it felt that way, all the same. Abandoned. Betrayed. Orphaned. Set adrift. Her internal thesaurus kicked in.

God, I don't understand. It feels like my life is falling apart. Wasn't writing Your plan for me? I thought so. Was I wrong? Or are You telling me that writing was only for a time?

She blinked away unexpected tears and picked up another panel, glad she had something to hit with the hammer. And by the time she'd driven the panel into the ground, she had regained control of her emotions. She could turn, look at the two Fullers, and smile as if everything were right with her world.

Fraud that she was.

"Hey," she said to Tom and Shauna, now working on their final panels. "Let's treat ourselves to cupcakes. It's Saturday. I'm buying."

Tom grinned but shook his head. "You won't be paying for anything. You volunteered for this installation. Besides, you bought last time."

"Okay. I'm not fool enough to argue. You're buying. Now my only problem is to decide which flavor I want."

Scruffy ran up and sat before her, as if he'd understood everything she'd said.

"I don't think there's variety when it comes to pupcakes," she told the dog in a stage whisper. "You'll have to settle for the same flavor, whatever it is."

Shauna laughed. "He doesn't care."

Tom finished the final installation, then stood back and surveyed the entire fence line. "Great job, crew. Scruffy won't be digging out again."

Shauna clapped her gloved hands together. "Let's go get cupcakes."

"Lunch first," her dad replied. "Then cupcakes."

The girl sighed dramatically.

Ignoring the theatrics, Tom asked Shauna, "Do you know where these hammers go?"

"Sure." She took both of their hammers and carried them, along with her own, toward the house.

Tom and Ariel followed at a slower pace.

"I appreciate your help today, Ariel. Made the work go a whole lot faster."

"I enjoyed helping. More fun than staring at a blank screen for hours." She closed her eyes, wishing she could call back the words.

"Book still not going well?"

She released a sigh. "Not going well. At all."

"I'm sorry. Wish I could help you in return, but I'm not a writer, especially of fiction. Shauna got that gene. Not me."

Ariel had the strangest urge to stop and give Tom a hug, to tell him help came in many forms. Even now, the call she'd received from Steven didn't seem as awful as it had awhile ago. And that was because of Tom and his daughter. Simply being with them made her feel better.

And maybe . . . just maybe . . . her improved spirits would cause creativity to return as well. Sooner rather than later. No doubt Steven would be asking about the status of her manuscript before he recommended another agent, and she didn't relish having to confess the truth.

CHAPTER 7

Tom welcomed Ariel to his classroom the following Wednesday morning. All of his students were present. No child out with a cold or the flu. And everyone seemed excited about meeting a published writer. He suspected a few—the boys, especially —would balk when they heard she was a romance writer. Understandably, most would prefer to hear from an author who wrote the type of books they liked to read. He silently prayed no one would say so aloud during Ariel's visit.

The previous night, Tom had printed off the bio from her website. Now he read it aloud to the class. Looking up from the paper in his hand, he added, "Remember to raise your hand when you want to ask a question. And be sure to introduce yourself when Miss Highbridge calls on you. First and last names. Okay?"

Heads nodded.

He glanced over at Ariel. "The floor is yours." Then he walked to a chair at the back of the room and sat down.

Ariel smiled at the students, appearing to look at each one of them before speaking. "How many of you like to read?"

Most of the kids raised their hands.

"How many of you like to write?"

Fewer hands went up this time. Shauna and her best friend, Lily Morley, seemed to be competing to see who could hold their arms the highest.

"I've always loved to read, but I haven't always loved to write. Even now, there are times I don't *love* to write. But I *always* love to tell stories. I love to tell about people and their emotions and the things they do that are heroic. But also the things they *shouldn't* do. I like to make readers feel happy and sad, even hopeful and anxious. And I like to introduce them to new people, or characters, and new ideas."

Tom looked at his daughter, seated on the opposite side of the classroom, and smiled at the rapt expression on her face. He could almost see the ideas churning in her head. It didn't matter to him if she won the festival prize or not. What he wanted was for her to try her best, whether it was writing or playing the piano or studying history or improving her marks in math.

"Can someone tell me what the theme is for the Christmas festival contest?"

Hands shot up and Tom returned his gaze to Ariel as she looked around the room, from student to student. At last she pointed at Olivia Fair, one of his sixth graders.

The girl sat up extra straight in her chair. "A Magical Christmas Eve."

"Oh, that's a great theme for your stories."

"I've already started mine," Olivia added.

"All the better. It's always best to start early so you have a chance to edit your story." Ariel looked around the room again. "Has anyone else begun?"

No hands went up. That surprised Tom. He'd seen Shauna writing in her bright yellow journal the last couple of evenings. He'd assumed she was already working on her contest entry. Apparently not.

"How many of you intend to enter?"

Eight hands went up in answer to Ariel's question. Tom felt a twinge of disappointment that all of his students didn't want to at least try. Last week, he'd considered making it a class assignment, then had decided against it. It didn't seem right to him. What if he gave a lower grade to an entry that went on to win the contest? Or a high grade to one that didn't win. No, better to let his students make their own choice in this instance. And he shouldn't be disappointed. Eight entries was better than half his class.

"Can you tell me what the word 'magical' means to you?" Ariel asked.

Hands went up again, and she received a number of answers to her question.

Ariel went on to talk about how to brainstorm ideas on paper, deciding if a story should be told in first person or third person, in present tense or past tense. Not all the kids in his class would understand everything she shared, but he appreciated that she didn't dumb down her comments but instead let the students ask more questions until they understood.

When the allotted time was up, Tom rose and went to

the front of the room. "Let's give Miss Highbridge our thanks."

Everyone applauded and a few shouted, "Thank you."

Afterward, Tom walked with Ariel to the classroom door. "I appreciate this more than you know," he said in a low voice. "You did a great job."

"It was fun." She offered a smile. "In fact, I feel inspired. I'm going to hurry home to do some writing of my own."

"Good for you. I hope the rest of the day goes great."

He watched until she disappeared around the corner of the corridor, then returned to his desk. "I hope you paid attention because we're going to spend the next half hour trying to put to use what Miss Highbridge taught us about storytelling. Take out your notebooks and pencils. Those of you planning to enter the contest, you may work on your story for the festival. The rest of you can write down ideas about any kind of story. Maybe make up a character and describe them. Or think about one of your favorite books and make up a story to go along with it."

Before he finished speaking, a few heads were already bowed over their composition notebooks, pencils scribbling away. A few others would daydream away the next thirty minutes and never make a single mark on the page. The remainder would give the assignment some modest attention, even if it didn't amount to much in the end.

As for Tom, he found himself wondering when he would get to see his neighbor again and admitting to himself that he hoped it would be soon.

WHAT MAKES CHRISTMAS MAGICAL?

Ariel stared at the question she'd typed on her laptop not long after returning home from the school. The cursor flashed on and off in the space after the question mark. She hit return and typed some answers.

Jesus.

Family.

Children.

Anticipation.

What if she wrote a Christmas story? She hadn't done that before. A Regency story set during the Christmas season. With a deadline in the spring, maybe that wouldn't work with her publisher's schedule. On the other hand, if she got into the Christmas spirit, maybe she could shake off this horrid inertia when it came to writing. Maybe she would become inspired and keep going and going and going.

She opened a web browser and typed *Christmas in Regency England*. She clicked the top suggestion and began to read. Halfway down the post, she stopped to write in her notebook: *Why not bring back a couple from a previous novel? Maybe they are married and have a child by this time? Maybe family and friends are coming together for Christmas, and they decide to play matchmaker for two of their visitors?*

Hmm. That might be fun.

Which of her couples should she bring back to life? What had been her most popular book? What hero and heroine had she received the most emails about? She opened a second browser window and went to her books on Goodreads.

Ariel's novels had appeared on some bestseller lists,

but she wasn't fooled into believing her stories would ever light the world on fire. While she wanted them to honor God, she also desired to entertain, to lift a burden, to bring a smile or mend something that was broken, to leave readers with hope in their hearts after the book covers were closed for the final time.

Slowly, she scrolled through some of the reviews on *Remembering the Duke*, paying particular attention to what readers had to say about Randolph Fredrick, Duke of Alderton, and Miss Barbara Foxdale. By the time Ariel read the last review, she was convinced this was the right couple to bring back for an encore.

Then again. She frowned. She'd had a few minor characters show up in more than one of her stand-alone novels, but she hadn't brought back any heroes and heroines as major characters in a later book. As blank as her mind had been the past few months, she would need to read her own novel again to refresh her memory. Were they—the duke and Miss Foxdale—as loved by readers as those reviews made her believe? Was the book even any good?

Which reminded her, Tom Fuller hadn't said anything about the copy of *Remembering the Duke* he'd purchased on Friday. He hadn't mentioned it on Sunday when they'd spoken briefly after church either. He hadn't mentioned it this morning when she was at school to talk to his class. Had he read it yet? And if so, did he like it or hate it? He must hate it. Why else would he have remained silent?

Maybe that was why she'd developed writer's block. Because she wasn't any good as a writer. Because the ten books that had been published over the past five years were all flukes—or worse. Maybe Bridget hadn't resigned after all. Maybe the publisher looked at Ariel's books and decided Bridget had made a huge mistake and fired her.

She remembered something Gwyneth had said in one of their video chats about two months ago. "Girlfriend, you're suffering from impostor syndrome." Ariel had laughed off the comment and quickly forgotten about it.

Now she typed in another search and got an answer: *Impostor syndrome, noun, the persistent inability to believe that one's success is deserved or has been legitimately achieved as a result of one's own efforts or skills.*

Hmm. Did she deserve the success she'd known? Had she legitimately achieved the publication of her books? And if so, then was she suffering from impostor syndrome? Would believing she deserved it get her over the writing hump?

She released a cry of frustration and hopped up from the desk chair. "What is wrong with me?" She walked down the hall to the bedroom, not even glancing at the photographs on the wall, then back to the living room. Once. Twice. A third time.

Be still. The whisper in her heart stopped her before she could retrace the route a fourth time. *Be still.*

"Be still and know that I am God," she said aloud.

She hadn't been still lately. She hadn't been truly still in a long while. For more than a year. Perhaps two years. Maybe longer. When was the last time she'd simply sat in God's presence, been with Him, listened to Him? When was the last time she'd been content to *be* and not to *do*?

"Lord, forgive me. I'm so sorry. I've been trying to refill the wrong well, haven't I?"

As soon as she said the words, she knew they were true. It wasn't the writing well that had gone dry. At least not first. It was her spiritual well that was empty. She closed her eyes and took a slow, deep breath.

The end of May. That was her deadline. And she could have the use of Gwyneth's house until then. What if she gave herself through New Year's Day to simply be and not do? Under normal circumstances, five months was ample time for her to write a novel. What if she spent more time quiet and still, allowing God to speak into her life? She could take long walks and get to see more of the island. Perhaps she could talk to Tom's students again. Doing so had made her feel happy . . . and less of an impostor.

She moved to the desk and stared down at the laptop screen. Taking a steadying breath, she quit the Scrivener document called "Untitled WIP." If ever there was a misnomer, it was calling that document a "Work In Progress." But perhaps, after a designated time away, it would become accurate at last. She closed the laptop, putting her computer to sleep.

CHAPTER 8

A riel left the house, a stocking cap on her head, a knitted scarf wrapped around her neck, and hand warmers in her coat pocket in case her gloves didn't do the job. She grinned up at the gray clouds moving swiftly overhead, feeling a sense of freedom she hadn't known in a long while. And to celebrate, she was returning to Cathy's Cupcakes.

"If this keeps up," she said aloud, "I'll weigh a ton before my stay in Sanctuary is over." Then she laughed and quickened her footsteps. Partly because the day was cold and windy. Mostly because it was almost two o'clock. She didn't want the shop to close before she got through the door.

As it happened, Ariel entered the bakery as an older woman—with a cap of short, gray curls and wearing an apron—was heading toward the door.

"You are just in time. But I'm locking the door behind you so no one else sneaks in." She turned the deadbolt. "Don't worry. I'll let you out again."

Ariel drew in a deep breath. The warm air in the shop was thick with the rich aromas of vanilla, nutmeg, cinnamon, and other spices she couldn't name.

"Is this your first time to my little bakery?" the woman asked. "I'm Cathy. Cathy Schuller."

"Lovely to meet you. I'm Ariel Highbridge. I'm staying in Gwyneth Muldoon's house until spring." She glanced toward the display which had fewer choices than her previous visits to the shop. "And this is not my first time to visit your bakery." She laughed softly. "I'm afraid I've become addicted in a very short period of time."

Cathy returned to the backside of the display case. "I should apologize for feeding a bad habit, but I'm afraid I can't. It wouldn't be good for business."

Ariel was tempted to place both palms on the glass, lean close, and stare at the remaining cupcakes inside, like a little child in a candy store. "I haven't tried the carrot cake yet." She pointed. "I'll take one of those and a caramel chocolate one." She straightened and met Cathy's gaze. "Do you have any pup-cakes left?"

"Sorry. I'm all out of those."

"Scruffy will be disappointed," she said beneath her breath.

"What kind of dog do you have?" The older woman reached for a white paper sack.

"Oh, I don't have one. It's my neighbor's dog."

Cathy paused as she reached for the carrot cupcake. "Tom Fuller's dog? Scruffy?"

Ariel nodded. "Yes. Scruffy's a big fan of your confections."

"Hmm." The woman placed the two cupcakes into the white sack and set it on the counter.

"Mrs. Schuller!" a voice called from the back. "Something's not right with this oven. Come quick!"

"Oh, sakes alive. Not again." Cathy disappeared into the kitchen, the door swinging behind her.

Ariel retrieved her debit card from the holder on her phone and waited for the woman's return. And waited. She couldn't leave without paying, but she didn't want to leave without the cupcakes either. And if she left, she wouldn't be able to lock the door behind her, meaning the front of the shop would be open to anyone and the cash register left unguarded. That didn't seem right. Not when Cathy Schuller had been so careful to lock the door after Ariel came in.

She took a step into the area behind the counter and display case. Undoubtedly it was a place for employees only. "Mrs. Schuller?" When there was no answer, she moved on until she reached the swinging door. "Mrs. Schuller?" She pushed cautiously on the door until she could look into the kitchen. Hot air swirled around her head, and a veil of smoke made her eyes water. "Is everything all right?"

"Yes. Yes, it's fine. There's no fire, if that's what you wondered. Just a batch of cakes burned to a crisp." Cathy stood, fists on hips, staring down at the floor. Behind her was the girl with pink hair who'd waited on Ariel the week before.

Ariel lowered her own gaze and saw a pan on the floor filled with the charred remains of what she assumed had been cupcakes.

"This old oven." Cathy gave the large appliance a harsh glare. "I thought it was repaired but I guess not. It's in worse shape than me."

"I've gotta go, Mrs. Schuller," the girl said, her tone snippy. "And you better get a new oven before this one burns the whole place down and you with it. I'm not gonna be back until it's fixed." She pulled the apron off and dropped it on the floor before leaving through the exit door at the back.

"Mercy me." Cathy seemed to wilt before Ariel's eyes. "That girl." She gripped the counter with one hand, steadying herself. "I think she means it this time."

"Here." Ariel walked across the kitchen. "Let me help you. You sit down on that stool. I'll take care of this." She grabbed a pair of oven mitts from the counter, then lifted the pan off the floor and carried it toward the sink.

"You're a godsend, Miss—" Cathy broke off, then said, "I'm sorry, dear. I clean forgot your name."

"Call me Ariel." She glanced over her shoulder to smile at the woman, now perched on a stool at the center worktable.

"Is Ariel a family name?"

She laughed. "No. I was named for the Little Mermaid herself. The one in the Disney film. My mom loved that movie and all the songs in it. But mostly she loved the romance." She turned back to the pan and scraped the burnt cakes into a trash can.

"It's very good of you to help me this way, Ariel."

"I'm glad I could. What's the problem with the oven?"

"The temperature control or some such. We set it for three-fifty, but then it goes on the fritz and who knows what the actual temperature is. My friends ask me why I don't close the place and retire. Maybe I should. I'm old enough. I'll be seventy-three in January. But if I retire, what would I do with myself? Having this shop keeps me in touch with the locals in the off-season, and I meet some very interesting people during the tourist season. When I work the front counter, that is."

Ariel went around the worktable, took the other stool, and drew it close to Cathy Schuller. "I've been on the island less than two weeks, but even I know your shop would be missed. Don't retire unless you truly want to."

"Then I suppose I must call the repairman to visit once again. I will soldier on."

Night had fallen over the island by the time Tom and Shauna followed the walk to the Bastida front door. Shauna hurried ahead of Tom and rang the bell. The door opened soon after, revealing Rick Bastida, Tom's best friend since first grade.

"Hey, Tom. Hey, Shauna."

"Are we the last to arrive?" Tom asked.

"You are, but you aren't late." Rick stepped back, opening the door wider. "Come on in."

For the past four years, on the second Wednesday of every month, Tom and Shauna had come to the Bastida home for dinner. Most months they were joined by Jon and Gina Carter, along with their two young daughters, Charlotte and Emily, as well as Dean and Faye Patrick, whose twin sons seldom came now that they were teenagers and too busy with other activities.

The Bastida home, located on the northeastern shore of the island, was a true showplace. Rick and his wife, Hallie, had built the house over a decade before. Their dream had been to fill the large house with children, a few by birth and others by adoption. But life had thrown them more than one curveball over the years, mostly because of Hallie's infertility followed by other health issues that had ruled out adoption.

Witnessing their faith hold strong in the midst of disappointment and heartbreak had strengthened Tom's own faith. He wouldn't have made it through the dark days before and after Christina's death without them. He was sure of that, and he thanked God for them in his prayers on a regular basis.

When Tom and Shauna entered the dining room, he found the full Wednesday night crew present. All four Carters. All four Patricks. Add in the Bastidas and the Fullers, and they had a party of twelve around the table. Beyond the wall of glass that faced the lake, he saw nothing but inky blackness. No boat lights flickered on the lake tonight. But inside, the room was filled with light and laughter.

"So, what's new with you?" Rick asked Shauna while taking her coat.

"I'm going to write a story for the festival contest, and I hope Miss Highbridge will help me."

Tom turned toward his daughter. "Did you ask her for help?"

"Not yet. But I'm gonna."

"Would that be fair to the other kids who enter?"

Shauna screwed up her face in thought.

"Who's Miss Highbridge?" one of the Patrick twins asked.

"The lady who's staying in the Muldoon house," his brother answered. "Duh. We met her at church. Remember?"

"Oh, yeah. The pretty one."

The pretty one. Tom couldn't agree more, and he wasn't surprised that two teens on the brink of becoming young men had noticed it too.

"You'd better sit down," Rick said, his hand landing lightly on Tom's shoulder. "Hallie's got dinner ready to serve."

Tom gave himself a mental shake and moved to oblige. He sat at the end of the table with Shauna on his left. Rick led them in a word of thanks for the food and the hands that prepared it, and before long, platters and bowls were circling around the long table and the buzz of conversation and laughter filled the air.

A number of conversations came and went before Rick looked at Shauna and said, "Tell us about this story you're writing for the festival."

"It's called 'A Magical Christmas Eve.' That's what everybody's story is called. And then it's up to the writer to figure out what magical means. At least, that's what Miss Highbridge said at school today. Dad had her come talk to us."

Rick gave Tom an inquiring look.

His defenses went up. "Gwyneth suggested it."

"Did she now?"

"She did."

Rick laughed.

What was his friend implying? Tom speared a forkful of green beans and put them in his mouth so he'd have an excuse for silence. Was his growing attraction for Ariel Highbridge that transparent?

CHAPTER 9

T om was taking out the garbage on Friday evening when he heard Ariel call his name. He looked first across the four-foot fence that separated their front yards, but he didn't see her, despite the bright porch light.

"Trash duty?" she asked, pulling his gaze to the sidewalk in front of their homes. She was just a dark shadow there.

"Yeah." He walked toward her.

"Which is a subject I need to ask about."

"Trash duty?"

"Yes. What exactly do we do with our trash? I haven't seen any garbage trucks. What do I do when my can is full?"

"Ah. Gwyneth should have left that info for you."

"That's what I thought."

"We haul our trash to the landfill ourselves. Everybody has to. People without vehicles get help from their neighbors. The landfill is on the north side of the island, not too far from the boundary to the state park. Some residents use their snowmobiles for trash duty in the winter. Most take it in the trunks of their cars or back of their trucks. That's what I do. I can take yours the next time I go. I'll plan on it for the rest of your stay on the island."

"Thanks. It makes me feel like a spoiled city girl. I'm used to trash pickup every Tuesday, come rain or come shine." She shivered and pulled her coat more tightly around her. "Can't believe how cold it is tonight. Feels like it could snow."

"Shauna and I are about to have a mug of hot chocolate. Care to join us? Great way to ward off the cold."

"That sounds good. I'd love to."

A thrill of pleasure rolled through Tom. He hadn't known how much he wanted her to accept the spontaneous invitation until it happened. It had only been a couple of days since she'd made her presentation to his class, but it seemed much longer since he'd seen her.

"Come on in." He motioned toward the door. "Shauna will want to talk to you about her Christmas story. She works on it every day after we get home from school."

"Good for her."

He was tempted to ask how her own writing was going, but decided against it. Why bring up bad feelings if it still wasn't going well?

"Miss Highbridge!" Shauna grinned and immediately reached for another mug. "You gonna have hot chocolate with us?"

"I would love to if you have enough."

"We've got plenty. It's just the instant stuff. Dad lets me make it." Shauna lowered her voice. "I always put in more of the powder than what it says to on the container. It's better that way."

"More chocolate is always better," Ariel whispered in return, casting a conspiratorial glance in Tom's direction.

He wondered again about a boyfriend back in Boise. Did she have one? And if not, why not? Look at her. Summoned by his own thoughts, the Patrick boy's voice repeated in his head. *"Oh, yeah. The pretty one."*

The electric kettle beeped three times.

"It's ready, Dad."

He moved to the counter and carefully poured the boiling water into the three waiting mugs. Shauna followed right behind with a spoon for stirring.

"Don't splash any of that hot water on your hand," he cautioned as he returned the kettle to its base.

"I *know*, Dad. You say that *every* time."

His back to her, he couldn't see his daughter's eye-roll, but he heard it in her tone.

Ariel laughed. Obviously, she'd heard it too.

He was growing more than a little fond of the sound of her laughter.

She doesn't live on the island. This is temporary. She might have a boyfriend back home in Idaho. I don't want Shauna to get hurt. My life is in Sanctuary. So is Shauna's.

Those were only a few of the reasons it shouldn't feel this right, this comfortable, with the three of them gathered in the kitchen, talking and laughing. But it *did* feel right. And Tom wanted to enjoy it for as long as he could.

~

ARIEL SAT at the Fuller kitchen table, both hands wrapped around the mug of hot chocolate. She felt at home, as if she belonged in this very spot, and it made her realize she hadn't known such a sense of belonging in a while. Perhaps the loneliness had begun with her dad's death. Or perhaps it had begun after her mom, Patricia, married Wes Sherman and moved to Bethlehem Springs in the mountains north of Boise. Or, more likely, perhaps it had begun with her cheating ex-boyfriend.

She lifted the mug to her lips and took a sip with her eyes closed. When she opened them again, she saw Shauna watching her, a chocolate mustache gracing the girl's upper lip. And just like that, the darker thoughts of a moment before vanished.

"Hey." Tom clicked his fingers. "I forgot something." He rose from the chair and went to a cupboard. On the top shelf, he grabbed a green and white box. From it, he withdrew three candy canes. "Stir your hot chocolate with one of these."

"Dad! Thanks!"

"Yes," Ariel joined in. "Thanks."

They removed the plastic wrap from their candy canes, and before long, each of them swirled the canes in their hot chocolate, watching as they melted away.

Finally, Shauna pulled the remains of her candy cane from the mug and put it in her mouth. "Mmmm."

Ariel mimicked her. The wonderful combination of chocolate and peppermint came alive in her mouth. "Oh, my. Where have I been? Why have I never done this before?"

Tom grinned, and something about his expression made her feel giddy on the inside.

"This time of year," he said, "there is one beverage I like even better."

"Better than this? What is it?"

Shauna raised her hand, as if she were in class. "I know. I know."

"Shh." Her dad put a finger in front of his lips. "Give Miss Highbridge a chance."

"Hmm…" Ariel leaned forward. "Hot or cold?"

"Hot," Shauna almost shouted.

"Hmm. Hot buttered rum?"

Tom shook his head.

Shauna asked, "What's that?"

"I don't know," her dad answered. "I've never had it."

"Teetotaler?" Ariel asked.

He nodded.

Shauna wrinkled her nose. "What's *that*?"

Tom laughed. "I'll explain it later."

Ariel racked her brain. He couldn't love warm milk better than hot chocolate with a candy cane mixed in. What other hot beverages were there? Coffee. Tea. Those were rather ordinary, even if she did enjoy both. "I give up."

"Hot apple cider," Tom said.

"With cinnamon sticks," Shauna chimed in. "Dad uses the slow cooker and I put the cinnamon sticks in, and then it just warms up and makes the whole house smell good. Doesn't it, Dad?"

"It sure does."

In unison, they picked up their mugs. The hot chocolate was no longer steaming hot and sipping wasn't required to avoid burning the tongue. Ariel listened as Shauna slurped the last of her beverage.

"Can I have more, Dad?"

"*May* I have more, and the answer is no. One's enough."

Shauna sighed as she stared into the empty mug in her hands.

Again the feeling of belonging swept over Ariel. What a perfect way to end the day, drinking something delicious with these two.

"I've been working on my story, Miss Highbridge."

She focused her gaze on the girl. "Have you? That's wonderful. What's it about?"

Shauna looked toward her dad, then back at Ariel. "Sorta about my mom."

Ariel sensed Tom's surprise but didn't glance his way.

"Mama loved Christmas. Didn't she, Dad? I remember she said nobody loved Christmas more than she did. She always made the house look really pretty. Red and green and white everywhere. Even the tree had red and green and white bows. And she baked lots of Christmas cookies to give to neighbors and friends at church and for the school. I got to do most of the frosting." Shauna stopped, her expression downcast. "I miss doing that with her."

"Of course you do," Ariel replied softly.

"Sometimes I forget what she looked like."

Ariel reached over and squeezed the girl's hand. She knew what that was like. Her dad's face often was hazy in her memory, and she'd been twenty when he passed away. Shauna was only seven when she lost her mother.

Tom cleared his throat. "Want to tell us more about your story?"

"Sure." Shauna brightened. "In my story, a mom and her little girl bake cookies on Christmas Eve and the little girl gets to frost them. Then her mom sends her to bed. It's after she's asleep that the magic happens."

Tom leaned forward, his forearms on the table. "What kind of magic?"

"I haven't figured that out yet." Shauna shrugged, completely unconcerned.

There was a moment of silence, and then Ariel laughed. If only she could be that nonchalant over not knowing what to write. But when she saw Shauna's stricken expression, she realized her error. "Oh, Shauna. I'm sorry. I wasn't laughing at you. It's just, I say the same thing all the time." She chuckled again. "I still haven't figured out my next story."

"Really?" Shauna's eyes widened. "I'm like you?"

"In that regard, you are."

"Cool."

Did all eleven-year-olds bounce between happy and sad, up and down, as rapidly as this girl? It made Ariel dizzy.

"Would you like to see what I've written?" Shauna asked.

Ariel glanced at Tom. "Would it be all right?"

He shrugged, then nodded.

Shauna bounced up from the chair and dashed out of the kitchen.

"She'd like you to help her," Tom said in a low voice. "But besides the fact that would be imposing on your time, she shouldn't have an advantage over the other kids, just because you're staying next door to us."

"I'll be careful."

Shauna returned, yellow journal in hand. With a smile, she placed it on the table.

Ariel lifted the book, opened the cover, and scanned the first page. Then she raised her eyes. "May I take this home to read it tonight? I'll return it to you in the morning before I go to the bakery."

"You're gonna get cupcakes again? Dad says we can't get them too often. They're kinda expensive on a teacher's salary. Huh, Dad?"

He gave a slight shrug but didn't comment.

"I'm not going there to *buy* cupcakes," Ariel answered. "I'm going to help *make* them."

Tom and Shauna looked at her in twin expressions of surprise.

Ariel laughed again. "I met Cathy Schuller on Wednesday. There was trouble with one of her ovens, and one thing led to another. Before I left, she'd offered me a job and I accepted."

A frown tugged at Tom's eyebrows. "I thought you came to the island to write."

"That's a story for another time." Rising from the chair, she glanced at Shauna and held up the journal. "For now, I'm going home to read something a friend of mine already wrote."

CHAPTER 10

Ariel's knock on the Fuller front door the next morning was answered by Shauna. Ariel passed her the journal. "You have a wonderful beginning. I especially like the part where Emma climbs onto Aslan's back without fear or hesitation. Keep going. I can't wait to read the entire story."

"You like it? Really?"

"Really."

"Cool."

Ariel looked up and saw Tom standing in the hall in his stocking feet. She smiled in his direction.

"Morning." He walked toward her. "You're up early."

"Have to get to Cathy's."

"That's right. I forgot. But before you go, I've got an invitation for you. My friends, the Bastidas—you met them at church. They want you to join them for Thanksgiving dinner at their place. Shauna and I will be there too."

"But I—"

"You gotta come with us," Shauna interrupted. "You can't spend Thanksgiving alone."

Tom put a hand on his daughter's shoulder. "She's right. You don't want to spend the holiday alone. You need to come. Turkey. Dressing. Mashed potatoes and gravy. Sweet potatoes. Cranberry salad. Pumpkin pie."

"Stop!" Ariel laughed. "You had me at turkey and dressing. Let me know what I can bring." She took a short step back. "I really must run. I don't want to be late on my first day."

She gave a little wave, then went down the steps and walked swiftly toward the center of town. Before she was halfway to the bakery, snow began to fall. Big, fat flakes at first, falling in a lazy dance. She stopped walking and turned her face skyward. Snowflakes barely touched her skin before they melted and were gone. Delight made her laugh. There was something about the first snowfall of the season that always put her in the holiday spirit.

"Thank You, Father. It's beautiful."

She hurried on. By the time she neared the back door of the bakery, the snowflakes were smaller, falling in a thick veil and blowing a little sideways. If it continued this way, she would be very thankful for her boots come the walk home.

She opened the rear door and stepped inside. Warmth enveloped her, along with delicious scents that made her mouth water. Her stomach wasn't empty. She'd taken the time to eat breakfast. But right at that moment, she wouldn't have turned down anything on Cathy's menu, with the exception of the pup-cakes.

"Good morning," she called as she removed her gloves and shoved them into her pockets.

Cathy glanced briefly in her direction. "Good morning."

"I'm not late, am I?" Ariel shrugged out of her coat, poked her knit cap into one sleeve, then hung the coat on a hook.

"No, you're right on time. I come in about 5:00. I enjoy being here by myself at first."

Ariel slipped an apron over her head and tied it around her waist. "Are you open more than two days a week during the tourist season?"

"Yes. But it's a lot for me to handle, and I haven't had the greatest success with employees. Every year I wonder if that season will be my last. Many of the younger folks go off to college and don't come back. It takes a special kind of person to take to island life, especially when the ferry stops running in the winter and doesn't start up again well into spring. Not until May, most years. Makes some folk restless, you know. Claustrophobic even."

Ariel wondered if that was how she would feel in a couple of weeks. Would she consider herself trapped? She'd grown up in the high desert of southern Idaho. Part of big sky country. She could get on the interstate and drive all the way to Portland, Oregon in about six or seven hours if she didn't have to stop. Six or seven hours without much congestion as there were only a few small cities and towns between Boise and Portland—and most of those places were bypassed on the freeway. Pedal to the metal and go. She knew because she'd taken that trip numerous times through the years. On this island, she didn't even have a car.

"But the locals," Cathy continued, unaware of Ariel's drifting thoughts, "we like the downtime winter brings. It's quiet and restful. Little bit of work, like my two days a week in the bakery. Kids in school, of course. But not much else going on."

"What about the Christmas festival?"

"That's for us. The locals. There are a few folks who fly over from the mainland, of course. And there are some residents who like to winter in Arizona who come back to be with family for the holidays. But for the most part, it's just the people who live on the island year round who go to the festival. A party for the family." Cathy wiped her hands on a towel, then motioned for Ariel to join her in the far corner of the kitchen.

The next couple of hours were filled with learning how to operate the mixers and ovens and where to find the various ingredients. Ariel's head whirled with information. She'd never considered herself a baker. But that morning, she felt a twinge of pride when she finished frosting her first two dozen carrot cake cupcakes and topped them with chopped pecans.

Cathy stuck her finger in the almost empty bowl, scooped up some remaining frosting, and stuck it in her mouth. "Mmm. Excellent job, Ariel."

"Thank you."

The older woman glanced toward a large clock on the wall. "I'd better show you how to check out customers."

"Me? I thought I was here to help in the kitchen."

"That was my intention, but it seems I need you out

front. Chloe meant it when she left the other day. She's not coming in."

"Chloe? With the pink hair."

"That's her."

Ariel's stomach tumbled with nerves. She loved her laptop and her Apple Watch, but she'd never used any type of point-of-sale device before. What if she made a mistake? Cathy would be busy in the kitchen, baking and frosting more cupcakes. Who would Ariel ask for help if disaster struck? It was a legitimate question. She didn't want misfortune to fall on the kindly owner of Cathy's Cupcakes because of her.

"I'm not sure that's a good idea," she said.

"Have you ever used an iPad?"

"Yes."

"Then you'll do fine. I'm not very techie, as my grandson likes to point out, and I can do it. Come with me, and I'll show you."

TOM STOOD with Rick Bastida while Dean Patrick unlocked the door to the storage unit, snowflakes falling silently around them. With a strong yank, Dean slid the door up, revealing the packed interior of the unit. Boxes of various sizes were stacked from floor to ceiling, and the walls were lined with giant candy canes, the ones that had hung from the lampposts in Sanctuary's town proper for the past twenty Christmas seasons. Maybe more.

"Looks a little more organized than usual," Tom said.

Rick chuckled. "Hallie was in charge of the teardown last year."

"Well, that explains it. Your wife is the most organized person on the planet."

Rick nodded. "She made sure all the boxes were labeled and kept in some kind of order. Decorations for the town square should be in one section. The light strings and garlands for the lampposts throughout town should be in another stack of boxes."

"Doesn't look like she left us much to do today."

Dean moved inside out of the snow that continued to fall. "Faye and Hallie are assigning volunteers to their various duties. No matter the weather next weekend, the decorations will go up. If the snow sticks around, we've got guys to pull sleds through town. And if the snow doesn't last for another week, we've got wheels to go onto the sleds and nobody'll need snowshoes to pull them."

"Not very many seasons we've needed the wheels," Tom commented as he and Rick also ducked inside the unit. "Snow is the rule."

"From the forecast, I'd say a white Thanksgiving is guaranteed." Rick opened the lid of a nearby box and glanced inside. "Which reminds me. Have you asked Miss Highbridge to join us for Thanksgiving dinner?"

"I did, and she's planning to come. Wondered what she can bring."

"Great. I'll have Hallie give her a call. I look forward to getting to know her."

After that, Rick handed clipboards to Dean and Tom, and the three of them completed the inventory of the decorations, an inventory Tom was certain would match whatever list Hallie Bastida already had at her home. By the time Dean closed and locked the unit's door again, at least three inches of snow blanketed the ground. The men said goodbye and headed off in three separate directions.

Tom meant to walk straight home. He had grading and lesson planning to do while Shauna played at a friend's house. He checked the time. Cathy's Cupcakes was only a couple of blocks away. He wondered how Ariel's first day had gone. He tried to picture her wearing a shop apron with her long hair tied up in a hairnet like Cathy wore when she was baking. But with Ariel's mesmerizing green-blue eyes, bright smile, and the musical laugh behind it, he couldn't imagine her as anything but beautiful. Hairnet or not.

Smitten. That was the term his mom would use to describe what he felt. She would say he was smitten with Ariel Highbridge, and she'd be right. Ariel had captivated his thoughts almost from the first moment they met, and his interest in her had caught him by surprise.

Over the past few years, Tom had become accustomed to life as a single dad. He adored his daughter. He loved being a teacher. He had good friends. He was part of a church that encouraged him and kept him accountable. He didn't *need* a woman in his life. And yet . . .

"Something's shifted inside of me, Lord. Is it wise for me to let myself care so much? Is this what You want for me?"

The awning over the entrance to Cathy's Cupcakes came into view, blurred by the falling snow. The storm seemed to have kept people home for the moment. There wasn't a line outside the bakery. Thankful not to have to wait, he went straight in, pausing long enough to stamp his boots on the large floor mat.

"Tom."

Pulse quickening, he looked up to find Ariel smiling at him from the other side of the counter. She wore the shop's logo apron, and her hair was caught up in what Shauna would call a messy bun. And she was just as pretty as he'd envisioned.

"This is a nice surprise," she added.

"I had some festival duties today and thought I'd stop by to see how you're doing. Didn't expect to find you out front."

"The girl who used to work the register quit."

"Chloe?"

"Yes. She walked out on Wednesday when there was a problem with one of the ovens. She didn't show up today."

Tom nodded. "She's done that sort of a thing before."

Ariel tipped her head slightly to one side. "Was she a student of yours?"

"Yes." He laughed. "If a kid lives on this island when they're ten or eleven, I've taught them. But trust me. The school is small enough I would know all of them anyway, even if they moved here as a teen. That's just small town life for you."

The door to the kitchen swung open and Cathy appeared. "Tom, I thought that was your voice."

"It's me. I don't think I've been in here on a Saturday when it's this quiet."

Cathy looked out the window at the falling snow. "It's unusual. For sure. But we'll have customers again as soon as the storm's over. What made you brave the snow?"

"Festival business. Rick Bastida and Dean Patrick and I were making sure the decorations are ready to go up around town next week."

"All the volunteers do a wonderful job." Cathy glanced toward Ariel. "Wait until you see it. The town becomes a winter wonderland. Right out of a Hallmark movie. Lights and candy canes and garland and evergreen boughs. But the snow is real. None of that fake stuff they use in Hollywood." She laughed, gave a small wave, and then disappeared into the kitchen.

Tom met Ariel's gaze. "Cathy's right. The town does look magical once the decorations are up."

"I can't wait to see it."

Tom couldn't help hoping he'd be the one who got to show it to her.

CHAPTER 11

Over the following week, Ariel felt the anxiety about her unwritten book lessen a little more each day. She rose by 6:00 AM, the sky as dark as ink beyond her windows, and sat on the sofa, a cup of hot coffee on the end table, her Bible open in her lap, and a small stack of other books beside her on the couch. Often something she read in the Word would send her to a commentary or to look up the meaning of the original Hebrew or Greek. Without the stress of needing to write a certain number of words on any given day, she gave herself freedom to follow as many rabbit trails as enticed her. A few mornings, she found herself still reading her Bible at 10:00 or even later. It was as if she'd been starving and hadn't known it until she began to eat. Then she discovered a little wasn't nearly enough to satisfy her hunger. She needed more and more.

In the afternoons, she took long walks around the town proper and down roads beyond the town boundaries, tromping through the snow, loving the pristine beauty of it all. Each walk made her fall a little more in love with Sanctuary Island. She saw children skiing to their homes at the end of the school day. She saw horses in paddocks, searching beneath the snow for a nibble of winter grass. She saw an occasional boat in the distance on the lake, a lake that was beginning to freeze along the shoreline.

On Saturday, Ariel was delighted to find Cathy had hired a new employee to work the front counter—a young man named Levi Carter. That left Ariel free to bake and decorate in the kitchen along with Cathy, something she much preferred. And as the day went on, she was especially thankful for Levi since the front of the bakery was more than a little busy, thanks to all the volunteers putting up the Christmas decorations throughout town.

Around 3:30, Levi poked his head into the kitchen. "We could use some more of those peppermint cupcakes. They're the most popular today." With that, he withdrew.

Ariel sprinkled more broken pieces of candy cane onto the frosted cupcakes he'd requested. "It's been some kind of crazy."

"It's always like this when the decorations go up. Plus it's sunny out, making everything so pretty after the storms. Why don't you take that tray of cupcakes to the front and then get on out of here so you can see things for yourself."

"My shift isn't over and besides, I couldn't leave while we're so busy. I can wait."

"Don't be silly." Cathy shooed with her hand. "The baking's done. I'll help Levi up front. Go on with you."

Ariel couldn't deny her eagerness to see the town decked out for the holidays. "If you're sure."

"I am. Go." Cathy waved her off.

Ariel grabbed the tray of peppermint cupcakes and headed for the front of the shop. As she slid the tray into the display case, the front door opened to let in another customer. Ariel looked up to see Tom and Shauna, both of them pink-cheeked from the cold and smiling at her.

She hadn't seen either of them for several days, and she realized how much she'd missed them.

"Hey, Miss Highbridge." Shauna hurried to the display case and placed her mittened hands against the glass.

"Hey, Miss Fuller," Ariel replied with a grin.

Tom came to stand behind his daughter, hands on her shoulders. "Glad to see there are cupcakes left. Shauna watched people coming and going from the shop all day and kept me informed about how busy it's been." He leaned down near the girl's right ear. "But what did I tell you before we came in?"

Shauna's eyes narrowed as she mimicked her dad. "This'll be the last cupcake until the Saturday before Christmas. Period."

Ariel laughed. "I think your dad's right. We have eaten a lot of them since I came to the island. Me included."

"But you *work* here now."

"You're right. I work here." She lowered her voice to a stage whisper. "Even more important for me to learn self-discipline and not to indulge more than I should."

When she looked at Tom, the approval in his gaze told her he appreciated her response. Warmth climbed her neck at his unspoken gratitude.

Tom pointed at the display. "We'll take two of those peppermint cupcakes, please. And I guess we'd better have some pup-cakes too."

Ariel glanced at Levi. "I'll get them."

As Ariel put the items in two small sacks, Tom said, "What time do you get off? Shauna and I wondered if we could show you around town. Especially the gazebo, now that it's ready for the season."

"I would love that," she answered without hesitation. "And actually, Cathy just told me to clock out. She wants me to see the decorations too."

"Great. We'll pay for those, and wait for you here."

"I won't be long."

Tom accepted the sacks from her. Then he and Shauna moved toward Levi, Tom's debit card in his hand.

As Ariel returned to the kitchen, removing the apron on her way, she wondered over the feelings flowing through her. It was more than simply that she'd missed seeing her neighbors for a few days in a row. It was an eagerness to spend time with them.

To spend time with Tom.

Her pulse stuttered at the thought. She liked him. She liked both Tom and his daughter. The pair had become good friends in a short amount of time. They'd made her feel less of a stranger on the island, and when she hadn't seen either of them for a few days in a row, she'd missed them. But Ariel's track record with the men she liked was abysmal. The last thing she wanted was to let her heart get attached to Tom or anyone else in Sanctuary. She would need to be careful.

Tom HELD the door open for Ariel and Shauna to pass through, then he followed them onto the sidewalk outside the bakery.

"My goodness," Ariel said, eyes wide. "It looks like everyone on the island is here."

Not everyone, but Tom guessed at least two hundred of the full-time residents of the island were walking through town, looking in newly decorated shop windows —even windows of shops that were closed until spring— and at lampposts where gold, silver, and red metallic garland sparkled in the late afternoon sunlight. Once the sun set in another hour, the tiny strings of lights would show, intwined as they were with the garland and around the large candy canes.

"Come see the tree in the town square." Shauna took hold of Ariel's hand. "I helped hang the ornaments on it while Dad did the lights on the gazebo with Mr. Bastida."

Ariel grinned "You were all very busy today."

Tom wished he'd reached for Ariel's hand before his daughter beat him to it. Only he didn't suppose they were at that place in their relationship yet where he should try to hold her hand.

Relationship? He was Ariel's neighbor, and he thought he could call himself her friend now. But did she want more than that? He did. That had become very clear to him over the past week. Trouble was, he'd been out of the dating game a long time. He hadn't asked a girl out in eighteen years. Not since he'd laid eyes on Christina while they were in college. And at the time they'd dated, they'd been on the mainland. There'd been lots of places to go and things to do. If he'd met Ariel in the summer, he would have had more options here on the island too—sailing, horseback riding, walking in the state park, attending plays, swimming in the lake, maybe even a game of golf although he wasn't very good at that. But it was winter. The ferry wouldn't run at all after next week, and any place here on the island that Tom might have considered a date possibility had shut down for the season. Well, there was The Lantern, but that restaurant was only open once a month this time of year.

"Dad!"

He had the feeling that wasn't the first time Shauna had called his name. He gave himself a mental shake. "What?"

"Tell Miss Highbridge about the tree this year." His daughter pointed at the large balsam fir on the east side of the gazebo.

"What about it?"

Shauna rolled her eyes. "How tall it is."

Obediently, he answered, "Nearly twenty feet tall."

Shauna and Ariel stopped walking, and Tom stepped up to Ariel's free side.

"Rick brought it back from the mainland yesterday," he said. "Most of us make do with artificial Christmas trees in our homes, but Sanctuary always has a real one in the town square."

Shauna looked up at her. "I like the way the real ones smell."

"Me too," Ariel responded.

Tom nodded. "I agree. But filling up our island land-fill with trees at the end of December every year isn't the best of ideas. Besides, bringing trees to the island is too expensive for most of us. Rick uses one of his company's trucks to transport the tree for the town square."

"I met Rick and his wife at church, but we didn't have time to talk for long. What does he do?"

"He owns a construction company in Havensport, although he builds in a number of different places, not just there."

"But he and Hallie live on the island year round?"

"Yes. Rick's got his own plane and his pilot's license. Makes the commute fast and easy." Tom heard someone call his name and turned his head to see who it was. "Speak of the devil." He grinned as he watched Rick and Hallie walk toward them. "Were your ears burning? We were talking about you bringing the big tree over to the island on one of your trucks."

"How tall is the tree?" Shauna piped up.

In unison, Tom and Rick answered, "Almost twenty feet tall."

Laughing, Shauna clapped her hands together, the sound muffled by her thick mittens.

"The town looks amazing," Ariel said. "It's hard to believe it was all done by volunteers, and in just one day."

Hallie replied, "Most of us have been helping with the decorations for so many years that we all know our duties." Her gaze swept the town square. "And now we get to enjoy it for the next six weeks. Then it will all come down until next year."

"It's all very special." Ariel smiled at Tom, as if he were special too.

It made him wonder if he might be special enough for something lasting to happen between them.

CHAPTER 12

Ariel leaned forward on the seat and stared through the windshield at the Bastida home. "Oh my," she whispered.

Tom turned off the engine. "It's really something, isn't it."

"It's almost a castle."

He laughed. "That might be a slight exaggeration."

"Well, a mansion anyway." Behind them, Ariel heard the clicking sound of Shauna unbuckling her seatbelt. She did the same, then got out of the SUV, shielding her eyes from the sun as she continued to stare at the enormous house made of wood and stone. Built into a hillside overlooking the lake, the house was surrounded by tall trees and what must be beautiful landscaping in the summer.

"Hallie and Rick designed the place themselves," Tom said as he came around to the passenger side of the vehicle. "Three stories with lots of bedrooms, a home theater, and more."

Ariel had known, of course, that wealthy people had

homes on the island. But her walks hadn't brought her out this far. Homes in and around the town proper were mostly older, smaller structures. The people who lived in them had simple lives and ordinary jobs. Many were only seasonally employed, earning the income they needed for an entire year when tourists flooded the island.

The Bastidas were not among the simple and ordinary.

"Come on." Tom cupped her elbow with his hand. "I can't wait for you to see inside."

If the backside of Rick and Hallie's home was impressive, it was nothing compared to the view the home had of Lake Huron through the wall of windows that made up the front of the home. Ariel had to concentrate to keep her mouth from dropping open in amazement.

"Welcome," Hallie said. "Please come in. Rick, take their coats."

The deeper into the house Ariel moved, the more delicious odors teased her nose. All the scents of Thanksgiving. However, while the calendar still read November, the expansive living room proclaimed Christmas was coming. A tall tree in a far corner sparkled with tiny lights and icicles. Wrapped presents were scattered around the tree skirt beneath it, along with stuffed bears, Santas, elves, and reindeer. A nativity set decorated one portion of a large entertainment center. Garlands of evergreen boughs and red ribbons draped the tops of the windows.

"This is so beautiful," Ariel said.

"Thank you." Hallie hooked an arm through Ariel's. "Come with me. I need to see to things in the kitchen, and I'd love to get to know you better."

"I'd be glad to help, especially since you wouldn't let me bring anything. I'm good at following orders."

Hallie's laugh was light and airy. "Thank you, but today you are a guest."

They moved from the living room, through the spacious dining room, and into the kitchen. It was all Ariel could do to keep from gasping out loud. The kitchen looked larger than her entire apartment back in Boise.

Hallie motioned toward a seating area at one end of the kitchen, an area meant—Ariel assumed—for guests to socialize while meals were prepared. "Make yourself at home." Then Hallie went to the top oven and peered through the glass on its door. "The bird's ready."

As if summoned by his wife's comment, Rick appeared in the entrance to the kitchen, Tom and Shauna right behind him.

"Sweetheart," Hallie said, "would you take the turkey out?"

"You bet." Rick grabbed a couple of oven mitts from the granite countertop.

Ariel's mouth watered. If the kitchen had smelled good before, it was ten times better once the roasting pan was out of the oven and set on the counter, the large bird browned to perfection.

"Yum," Shauna said, standing near the center island. "Look at it, Dad."

"I see. What can I do to help?"

"Nothing," Rick and Hallie answered in unison.

Hallie laughed. "Sit with Ariel and talk with us. Rick and I have this."

And the couple definitely had it. They moved around

the kitchen, dodging and circling each other in what looked like a practiced dance—carving the turkey, mashing the potatoes, making the gravy, pulling warm rolls from the oven, taking the cranberry salad from the fridge.

As Ariel watched Rick and Hallie, envy squeezed her heart. Once upon a time she'd dreamed of being one-half of a happy couple. She'd believed romance would grow and lead to love and marriage and family. But her heart had been wounded one time too many, it seemed. And she'd stopped believing in happily ever afters.

Her gaze shifted to Tom as he said something to Rick.

She *had* stopped believing. Hadn't she?

TOM HAD BEEN to enough Thanksgiving dinners at the Bastida home to know when it was time to rise from a chair and join a circle in the kitchen for the blessing. As he stood, he held out a hand for Ariel. A look of surprise flashed in her eyes before she took it.

Rick said, "Tom, would you do the honors?"

"Sure." He squeezed his daughter's right hand with his left and almost did the same to Ariel with his right, stopping himself at the last moment. Head bowed and eyes closed, he prayed, "Father God, we thank You for this wonderful feast Rick and Hallie have prepared for us. Bless them for their servant hearts, for opening their home to us this Thanksgiving Day. Help us to, in turn, reach out with hands of friendship to those we meet. May we reveal Christ to them in all we do and say. Lord, we ask that You would stir our hearts in gratitude. Help us to be content whether we find ourselves in plenty or in want. Help us to remember that little is much if You are in it. May we be a blessing to those around us, by our actions and by our words and perhaps even by our silence. Teach us to dwell upon things that are true and honorable and right and pure and lovely and of good repute. And, Lord, let us remember every single day to be a thankful people. Fill us with grace and gratitude. In Your name we pray, Amen."

"Amen," the others echoed.

Tom looked up and smiles were exchanged.

Hallie motioned toward the end of a counter. "Plates are there. Dish up and then find your place at the table."

Shauna was quick to obey, and Tom followed behind her.

The next hour and a half was filled with good food and pleasant conversation as well as lots of laughter. The Bastidas asked Ariel questions about her writing career and her home in Idaho, and they in turn answered her questions about their life on the island. Listening, Tom felt the rightness of the moment. Ariel didn't seem like a guest but a well-loved friend. She fit at this table the same way his hand fit in his driving gloves. Perfectly. The same way Christina used to fit. That thought tasted bittersweet, yet it filled him with hope at the same time. It felt as if Ariel belonged in his life, the way Christina once belonged.

Putting the final bite of pumpkin pie with whipped cream into his mouth, Tom said, "Hallie, that was amazing. As always."

"Thank you." She beamed. "Feeding others is one of my love languages."

"I know. I've been one of the lucky recipients for years."

Ariel pushed back her chair and stood. "You cooked. I'll do the cleanup."

"No, you won't," Hallie replied, also rising. "You're our guest."

"A guest who insists on helping."

A short while later, after the two women and Shauna had disappeared into the kitchen, hands full of dirty dishes and table service, Rick leaned forward and said in a low voice, "I like her."

"So do I."

"I can see that. It's written all over you."

"Is it?"

"Yes."

Tom swirled a finger tip on the white tablecloth. "There's a lot that could go wrong. I mean, I live in Michigan and she lives in Idaho."

"Yeah, that's a fact."

"And there's Shauna. She could get her hopes up that Ariel will stay, that there'll be something permanent between us. Then her hopes could be dashed if Ariel leaves."

"That's true. And your hopes could get dashed, too." Rick watched him with a sympathetic gaze.

Tom felt a weight of apprehension pressing on his chest. "Yeah, they could."

"Place it in God's hands, Tom."

He knew Rick was giving good advice. Faith demanded he trust God for what was best. But he'd trusted God for Christina's healing and she'd died anyway. Oh, he knew she'd been healed and made whole when she stood in the presence of her Savior. But that hadn't stopped the pain of losing her, of missing her. What if he opened his heart to Ariel, only to find she wasn't in God's plans for him? There would be more pain, more missing. Was it worth the risk?

As if in answer, an old hymn—one of his grandmother's favorites—sprang into his mind. *I am weak, but thou art strong,/ Jesus, keep me from all wrong;/ I'll be satisfied as long/ As I walk, let me walk close with Thee.*

The lyrics soothed him. He was weak. God was strong. He only needed to trust and be satisfied with walking with Jesus, no matter what.

Water ran in the kitchen sink. Dishes clattered. Silverware clanked. Voices hummed, punctuated with laughter. Homey sounds. Contented sounds.

Tom rubbed his face with one hand. "I keep going around Mount Sinai, picking up the same problem and giving it back again."

"You aren't alone. Just like the Israelites, it seems we all end up repeating experiences or challenges because we didn't learn the necessary lesson the Lord wanted us to learn." His friend took a sip from the water glass in front of him. "I've done the same. I had plenty of questions when we discovered we wouldn't have a bunch of kids to fill this house. I wanted answers from God. I demanded answers. I didn't get them. Not all of them anyway. Like 'If you ask Me anything in My name, I will do it.' I asked for children in His name, but I didn't see it happen. How come?"

Tom knew it was a rhetorical question, but he answered anyway. "Prayer doesn't always change circumstances, but it does change the person who prays faithfully."

"More of your grandma's wisdom?"

"Yes. And my mom's and dad's."

"Lucky you."

Tom smiled. "Yes."

His friend leaned forward a second time, forearms on the table. "Don't stop living, Tom. We get hurt in life. We're promised there will be trouble because we live in a fallen world. But that doesn't mean we quit living. We persevere."

"'And not only this,'" Tom quoted, "'but we also celebrate in our tribulations, knowing that tribulation brings about perseverance; and perseverance, proven character . . .'"

Rick joined in. "'. . . and proven character, hope; and hope does not disappoint, because the love of God has been poured out within our hearts through the Holy Spirit who was given to us.'"

"Amen," Hallie said from the dining room entrance. Then with a smile she asked, "Did you two decide to have church without us?"

"Ya snooze, ya lose," Rick answered.

Ariel and Shauna appeared at Hallie's side, his daughter looking up at Ariel with adoring eyes. A sense of peace and happiness warmed Tom's heart, and the feelings drove away doubt, at least for the moment.

"Let's move to the great room," Hallie said.

Tom rose from his chair, but he didn't step away from the table. Not until Ariel approached him and he could fall in beside her. Together they moved toward the great room.

"Dad! Stop!"

Startled by Shauna's demand, both Tom and Ariel stopped still, and he saw his daughter pointing to a spot above his head. He looked up to find mistletoe hanging from the archway.

"You gotta kiss her, Dad."

He lowered his gaze to look at Ariel. She watched him with widened eyes, perhaps as surprised as he at the demand. But could she know how much he wanted to oblige his daughter? He would like nothing more than to taste her lips with his own. Should he kiss her? Shouldn't he?

His hesitation lasted too long. She rose on tiptoes and kissed his cheek, then moved away from him before he could decide what to do. His hesitation was something he would remember and regret throughout the remainder of that Thanksgiving Day.

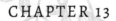

CHAPTER 13

GWYNETH:

Good morning. How was your
Thanksgiving?

ARIEL:

Good. Went to Rick and Hallie Bastida's
home with Tom and Shauna. Lovely day.

GWYNETH:

Lovely, huh?

ARIEL:

Yes.

GWYNETH:

Glad you weren't alone.

ARIEL:

Me too.

GWYNETH:

You seeing a lot of Tom?

ARIEL:

Not a lot. Some.

GWYNETH:

How's the writing?

ARIEL:

Not writing. Taking time off from it.

GWYNETH:

???

ARIEL:

It's okay. God's trying to get my attention. Much to ponder.

GWYNETH:

So what are you doing to fill your time?

ARIEL:

Working at Cathy's Cupcakes.

GWYNETH:

🧁 ?

ARIEL:

Loving it. Loving Cathy too. Interesting woman.

GWYNETH:

Full of surprises, girlfriend.

ARIEL:

Try to be.

GWYNETH:

Explored much of the island?

ARIEL:

Some. Pretty with snow and decorated for Christmas.

GWYNETH:

Agree.

ARIEL:

Will send photos.

GWYNETH:

Do that. Must run. Black Friday shopping to do.

ARIEL:

Crazy. No such thing here, even if I wanted to. Don't want to.

GWYNETH:

I know. Talk soon. Bye.

ARIEL:

Or is it, buy?

GWYNETH:

😊😊😊

～

Ariel placed her phone on the end table, then picked up the book she'd been reading when the ping of Gwyneth's first message interrupted her. But her interest in the book had waned already. Her eyes went instead to the living room window while her thoughts returned to yesterday.

"You gotta kiss her, Dad."

Her heart skittered as Shauna's words echoed in her memory. For a few breathless moments, she'd thought Tom *would* kiss her. What would Gwyneth think if she'd shared that information? Instead of answering the question, *"You seeing a lot of Tom?"* with *"Some,"* Ariel could have answered, *"He almost kissed me."* But had he almost kissed her? Or had she imagined it?

Real or imagined, she'd *wanted* him to kiss her. She'd wanted it far too much.

Ariel rose from the sofa and walked to the window. Snow had begun to fall again. Lazy flakes, drifting toward earth. Beyond the fence separating her yard from the Fuller yard, she saw Shauna rolling a ball of snow. For a snowman, she assumed. Scruffy ran into view and raced around the girl. Closer to the fence, Tom rolled another large ball of snow.

Like a movie playing on a screen, she remembered herself as a girl of ten, making a snowman with her dad in the small park near their home. Laughter sang in her memory, and she smiled even as a lump formed in her throat. Oh, how she missed her dad. He'd been gone over twelve years, but sometimes it felt like only yesterday that she'd received the awful news of his heart attack.

She blinked away the memories in time to see Tom looking in her direction. When their gazes met through the glass, he raised his arm to wave at her. Caught watching the father-daughter moment, she couldn't do anything except wave back. Then Tom motioned with his hand for her to join them. There was no doubt in her mind and heart. She wanted to join the fun. She held up an index finger, mouthing, *One minute.* Then she rushed to get coat, hat, gloves, and boots. Not long after, she entered her neighbor's backyard, squeezing past the gate that would only open partway due to the deepening snow.

"Hey, Miss Highbridge."

"Hey yourself, Shauna."

Footprints ran the width and breadth of the yard where they'd packed down snow while stealing some for the snowman taking shape in the corner.

"I'm rolling the head," Shauna called as she returned to work.

Tom pointed. "If you brush the snow away near the steps, you should find some stones that are just the right size for eyes."

Ariel gave a little salute before walking toward the back steps. After finding two black stones—they would have been perfect for skipping on the lake—she turned in time to see Scruffy fly through the air and snatch a carrot out of Tom's hand.

"Scruffy!" he shouted, but the dog paid no attention as he raced toward the back porch.

"Dad, now we don't have a nose."

"Not to worry." Tom reached into his pocket and pulled out another carrot. "I brought a spare."

Shauna finished rolling the snowman's head, ending at its base. Stepping back, she allowed her dad to lift the head into place.

Sounding like a surgeon calling for a scalpel, Tom said, "Eyes."

Ariel obeyed, setting the stones in place. Before she could move away, Tom stepped to her side and set the carrot beneath the snowman's eyes.

"What should we do for his mouth?" Shauna asked.

"How about marbles?" Tom put a hand on Shauna's shoulder. "There's a small bag of them in the middle drawer of my desk."

"I'll get 'em." The girl darted off toward the house.

"What about some branches for arms?" Ariel suggested.

"Great idea."

They turned in unison toward a large sycamore tree.

Tom said, "The last windstorm brought down some smaller branches. We ought to be able to find something beneath the snow near the fence."

By the time Shauna returned with the bag of marbles, the snowman had sprouted two crooked arms but looked desperately in need of a smile. Scruffy, on the other hand, seemed to think Frosty needed to lose his nose. Running ahead of Shauna, the dog leaped toward the snowman. Tom caught him in mid-air, then lost his balance and tumbled to the ground, dog in arms. Shauna giggled, and Tom released his hold on the dog and grabbed his daughter around the legs, bringing her down on top of him.

"You two are crazy," Ariel said, laughing at their antics.

"Is that right?" Tom's arm shot out a second time, grabbing her ankle.

With a cry of alarm mixed with delight, Ariel landed in the fluffy snow beside Tom and Shauna. "No fair!" She rolled her head to the side and found Tom watching her. Watching her from mere inches away. The breath seemed to leave her lungs, refusing to return, and the warmth in his eyes mirrored the heat suddenly whirling in her belly. "No fair," she repeated in a whisper.

Would he kiss her this time?

"Dad!"

Tom blinked—as if just remembering his daughter was

with them—before rolling his head toward Shauna. A moment later, he rolled it back again, a wicked grin curving the corners of his mouth and mischief replacing heat in his eyes. "Everything's fair in a snowball fight."

"This isn't a snowball fight," she replied.

"It should be."

Accepting the unspoken challenge, Ariel scrambled to her feet and rushed across the yard where she scooped up a heap of snow and shaped it into a ball. Turning, she saw Tom's look of surprise a second before she tossed the rounded missile. It hit him square in the chest.

His surprise lingered only a moment before his laughter rang out. That was followed by a frenzied making and tossing of snowballs by all of them, save for Scruffy and Frosty.

THAT EVENING, Tom sat on Shauna's bed and tucked the blanket and comforter over her shoulders.

"Dad, I like Miss Highbridge."

"So do I."

"You laugh more when she's around."

"Do I?"

"Yes."

"I didn't know that." He bent forward and kissed his daughter on her forehead.

Shauna yawned before rolling onto her side, loosening the bedcovers.

Love swelled in Tom's chest, and he said a silent thanks to God for giving him this precious girl.

"Hey, Dad?"

"Hmm?"

"I finished my story." Eyes closed, she pointed toward the bedside table. "You can read it if you want to."

"I want to," he answered softly.

"Okay." Shauna's voice was muffled by the comforter she'd pulled up next to her face. "Bring it back in the morning."

"You've got it, Peanut."

"Maybe I'll be a writer like Miss Highbridge."

"Maybe you will." He ruffled her hair. "Maybe you will."

As he stood, he picked up the yellow journal with his right hand, then made his way out of the bedroom, turning out the bedside lamp on his way. He took the time to make himself a cup of herbal tea, then he settled into his favorite chair and opened the journal, smiling as he looked at his daughter's familiar handwriting.

A Magical Christmas Eve by Shauna Fuller

In the cozy little town of Snowflake Cove, there lived an eleven-year-old girl named Emma. Emma's favorite book was *The Lion, the Witch, and the Wardrobe* by C.S. Lewis, and from the time she was really little she dreamed about meeting Aslan the Lion. She knew it would be the coolest thing ever.

One Christmas Eve, she baked cookies with her mama and helped to frost them. Emma and her mama did that together every year, and Emma thought it was the funnest thing ever because she loved her mama so much. And they talked and laughed a lot while they mixed and baked and frosted cookies.

Later that evening, Emma went to her bedroom. She was supposed to go to sleep, but instead she sat by the window, reading her favorite book. When she looked up from its pages, snow was falling. Everything outside looked pretty because of it. Softly she whispered, "I wish I could go to Narnia." Just before the clock struck midnight, a soft glow filled her room, and a mysterious figure appeared out of the shadows. As the figure stepped forward, she realized it was Aslan, as awesome as she'd always imagined him to be.

"Emma." The great lion's voice was powerful and gentle at the same time. "I have come to take you on a journey this Christmas Eve. Join me now."

Without hesitation, Emma climbed onto Aslan's back. The lion took a big leap and Emma held tight to his mane as they soared through her open window and into the night sky, leaving a trail of stardust behind them. They flew over snowy mountains and icy rivers until they reached a land where Christmas trees touched the sky and candy canes grew like flowers in her mama's garden. This was a part of Narnia Emma hadn't read about in any of the books or seen in any of the movies either. It was all brand new to her. Everything except Aslan himself.

Aslan took Emma to a grand castle made of gingerbread and icing. There they were greeted by elves who were busy preparing for Christmas.

"May I help?" Emma asked eagerly.

"We would love your help," one of the elves answered.

Emma began to wrap presents. She worked for hours but she never got tired or sleepy.

Suddenly, a cold wind swept through the land. The Ice Witch, who despised the joy that came with Christmas, had cast a spell to freeze Christmas Eve in time so it would never become Christmas Day. The elves huddled in fear, but Emma decided to go with Aslan to stand up to the witch.

Aslan and Emma journeyed through the forest to the Ice Witch's hiding place. The witch sneered at their arrival. "You cannot stop me, little girl. Christmas Eve will be frozen forever! You will never see Christmas again."

But Emma, with a heart full of Christmas spirit, bravely stood before the witch. "You cannot freeze it forever. Christmas is about love and joy. Christmas is about family and friends. Christmas is about helping others. Christmas happens because of how much God loves us. That's why Jesus was born in that stable. He came to show God's love to everyone. When that truth lives in people's hearts, you can't freeze it! It warms their hearts and that warmth melts a frozen world."

Touched by Emma's words, the Ice Witch's own icy heart began to thaw, and with that, the spell over Narnia thawed too. The land blossomed into a beautiful winter wonderland as the clock turned from Christmas Eve to Christmas Day.

Aslan roared triumphantly, and the elves cheered. The Ice Witch, now full of Christmas joy, joined them in celebrating the true meaning of Christmas.

As dawn approached, Aslan said, "It is time to return home, Emma. Remember, the joy of Christmas is something to share with others. Never keep it to yourself."

Emma awoke in her bed, the first light of Christmas morning peeking through her window. She smiled, certain her journey to Narnia hadn't been a dream. She had lived a magical Christmas Eve adventure, one she would remember forever.

And so, in the little town of Snowflake Cove, Emma's Christmas was filled with extra joy, all thanks to her journey with the gentle but mighty Aslan on a magical Christmas Eve.

The End

With a smile, Tom closed the journal. He might be prejudiced, but he had to believe this would be the winning entry in this year's festival contest. He'd found it charming and quite well written too. Who knew his little girl had such a vocabulary? Maybe Shauna really would grow up to be a novelist.

He picked up his phone. Almost nine o'clock. Was that too late to call Ariel? He would like to tell her about the story. Maybe read it to her. After all, it wasn't very long. Perhaps five or six hundred words at most. Or would it be better for her to read it alone? He didn't want to unduly influence her to feel one way or the other about it.

Oh, who was he trying to fool? Shauna's story was just an excuse to talk to Ariel. About anything at all. They'd had fun today building a snowman and having a snowball fight. He'd hated it when she excused herself and went home. Hated it.

Next time his lips were mere inches from hers, as they had been when he and Ariel were lying in the snow, he wouldn't hesitate. He would kiss her. Mistletoe not required.

CHAPTER 14

T om lay on his back on the kitchen floor of his elderly neighbor, his head and shoulders inside the cabinet beneath the sink.

"I don't know what I'd do without you, Tom Fuller," Stephanie Boyland said in that wispy voice of hers.

"I'm always glad to help if I can." Tom gave the wrench another unnecessary tug. "I don't think you need to worry about a leak. There's no sign of one anywhere." He slid out from under the cabinet, then sat up.

The tiny, stoop-shouldered woman leaned over and looked behind him. "I was so sure I heard a drip-drip-drip."

"Well, there's no dripping now." He got to his feet.

"Will you stay and have a cup of tea?" She turned on the burner beneath a tea kettle on the stovetop.

Tom suspected Mrs. Boyland had summoned him to her home for this moment, not because she'd actually thought there was a leak beneath her kitchen sink.

"I met your new neighbor." The woman pulled a stool

into place, then stepped on it to retrieve two cups from the lowest shelf of a cupboard. "I was in Cathy's Cupcakes the day before Thanksgiving. Oh, my. That place was busy. You'd think no one planned to make pumpkin pie, the way folks were buying those cupcakes. At least Cathy seems to have good help now. I worry she'll work herself into the grave. Most folks retire long before they're her age."

Tom listened while he put away the last of his tools.

"Pretty thing, isn't she?" Mrs. Boyland glanced his way, curiosity in her faded blue eyes.

"Who's pretty?" He leaned his backside against the counter.

"Ariel Highbridge. That's who we were talking about." She huffed before returning to her tea preparations.

"Yes, she is."

"Guy Williams told me she's a writer."

"She is. A good writer."

"Oh?" Mrs. Boyland faced him again. "You've read her books?"

"One of them."

"She didn't think you'd read it."

Had Ariel told Mrs. Boyland about him buying her book? Tom felt heat rise in his neck. *Remembering the Duke* was still on the stand next to his bed. He hadn't finished reading it yet. Not because it wasn't good. It was a well-written novel. Even he could see that. The story was both sweet and romantic. Not his usual reading fare, although it had held his interest. But for some reason, over the last couple of weeks, he hadn't picked it up again in order to read the final four or five chapters. Now he wondered why.

"Well," Mrs. Boyland said. "You should tell her what you thought of the book so she doesn't think you don't care enough to read it."

The kettle began to whistle.

Why hadn't he told Ariel what he thought of her book, even though he hadn't finished it yet? For that matter, why hadn't she asked him about it? She'd apparently mentioned it to Stephanie Boyland, so it must have been on her mind. Were her feelings hurt by his silence? That wasn't his intent.

He frowned in thought. Shauna had asked him about the novel a couple of times, too, but he'd answered that he would give it to her when he finished. Apparently writing her own story had been enough of a distraction to keep Shauna from bugging him again. But did Ariel know that?

He thought of her as she'd been yesterday, building the snowman, throwing snowballs. She hadn't seemed hurt or offended by his silence about her writing. The same with Thanksgiving Day at the Bastidas. Still, why would she have said something about him and her book to a woman she'd only just met in a cupcake shop? Did that make sense?

"Have a seat." Mrs. Boyland lifted a tray holding the cups of tea, some lemon slices, and a sugar bowl.

Tom followed her to the small kitchen table, sitting opposite her.

"Stop frowning, Tom. The course of true love never did run smooth."

Instead of vanishing, his frown deepened. "I believe you're getting ahead of yourself, Mrs. Boyland."

"Am I?" She placed the tip of her right index finger against her nose. "My mother always said I have a nose for romance."

"When was that?"

"Nineteen forty-four, if I'm not mistaken. I knew the man my sister would marry the minute I met him. And I told my mother and sister. My sister said it would never happen, but they married the month after V-E Day." She grinned. "They gave me six nieces and nephews as part of the baby boom."

Tom knew Mrs. Boyland and her husband had never been blessed with children. Her sister's children and grandchildren and—if there were any—great-grandchildren were the only family she had. "Where are all those nieces and nephews now?"

Her smile vanished. "Some dead. The rest of the family is scattered to the wind."

"Do any of them come to visit you?"

"Why would they? Most of them have never met me. And I'm old and uninteresting."

Tom's heart pinched at the answer, spoken in such a matter-of-fact tone. He aimed for levity. "Oh, I don't know about that. I think people just get better with age." That much, at least, was true.

Mrs. Boyland stirred her tea with an undersized spoon. "I've had a good life, Tom Fuller, and with neighbors like you, I've got no complaints."

"There is something to be said for the days when families stayed put and didn't move all over the country."

The elderly woman reached across the table. Her small hand was gnarled, misshapen by arthritis, the skin crinkled. "We get nostalgic about the old days, but those old days had their problems too. You remember that. Don't let nostalgia hold you back. Think about a future with Ariel Highbridge instead."

"I'll remember. And you remember to call me any time you think you hear a leak under that sink."

"Thank you, Tom. I'll do just that."

"SEE YOU AT CHURCH," Ariel called to Cathy as she left the bakery.

Although the shop had been busy, the town was quiet now. The fresh blanket of snow that had fallen yesterday glittered in the sunlight of late afternoon. It lay undisturbed in many places, but the narrow streets that crisscrossed the town proper were streaked with the tracks of cross-country skis.

"Maybe I need to give skiing a try," she said aloud.

Rather than head north on Main Street, she turned south and walked toward the bookstore. She hadn't revisited Whimsical Pages in the past couple of weeks, but she was ready to browse and buy today. A friend from her home church in Boise had told her about a book on hearing the voice of God, and it sounded perfect for this time in her life. If Guy Williams didn't have it on the store shelves, she would have him order it for her. And if all else failed, she would buy the ebook version so she could have it immediately.

When she entered the bookstore a short while later, Guy was ringing up an order for another customer. He glanced up and tossed her a smile, then returned to business. She moved down the aisle, looking for a Christian Living section. She eventually found a few Bibles and some commentaries, but there were very few other choices that fell under the category of Christian. Definitely not the book she'd wanted to find. Of course, it wasn't a new release, so she couldn't be surprised it wasn't in a bookstore that had limited space.

She moved on, letting her fingers trail over the spines of books, pausing every so often to pull one off the shelf, look at the cover, read the blurb on the back, then slide it back into its space. Soon enough she found herself in the fiction section, and to her great surprise, she saw several of her titles. Not only copies of *Remembering the Duke*, which had been in stock before her arrival on the island, but several of her older releases as well.

She glanced toward the front of the store, thinking what a nice thing Guy had done, ordering more of her books. Only kindness could be the reason. It wasn't as if she made a fortune from her writing. She was not an author whose name was known far and wide. Only the legacy from her paternal grandfather and strict budgeting allowed her to write full-time. She did well enough, but she would never get rich from her writing. And she was okay with that.

She chuckled softly to herself. *At least I try to be okay with it.*

She took one of her books and stared at the cover. Sales numbers, bestseller lists, and accolades were all great. The feeling she got when she saw one of her stories available in a bookstore—finished, edited, and published —was special. But it wasn't what should matter most to her.

Father God, draw me closer. Be my center.

After sliding her book into place, she returned to the small Christian section. She didn't need a new Bible, but she could give the other books a closer look. Perhaps God wanted one of them to speak into her life.

When I seek Him, I will find Him.

It seemed clear, in a deep corner of her heart, that God had brought her to Sanctuary Island for something more important than writing a novel. While she wanted her writing to please Him—and she thought it did—she sensed something more awaited her, if only she remained open to His leading.

And so she would.

CHAPTER 15

With the words of the pastor's inspiring sermon lingering in Tom's heart, he reached for his Bible on the pew beside him. He and Shauna had arrived late this morning. She'd hurried off to Sunday School while he'd slipped into the last row during the opening worship song.

As he stepped into the side aisle, his gaze swept over the congregation. He smiled and nodded as his gaze found friends and neighbors. He was always glad to see them, of course. These people were part of his family. His brothers and sisters in Christ. But when he saw Ariel in a pew near the front of the sanctuary, his heartbeat quickened, as if he hadn't seen her in a year instead of a mere two days.

He sidled up close to the wall, allowing others to pass by him while he kept an eye on Ariel. She smiled as she talked to Hallie Bastida. Two other women joined them—Meg Harlowe and Vicky Williams—and he supposed Hallie was making introductions. He liked that Ariel fit in on the island, that she was making friends, more friends than just him. He liked it because maybe it meant she would want to—

Abruptly, he broke off the thought, recognizing where it had taken him. Had he gone from cautious to reckless in as little as one month? It would seem so.

"You gotta kiss her, Dad."

Oh man. His daughter's heart seemed to want the same thing he wanted. The last few years, he'd sought to protect Shauna from caring too much for someone who wouldn't stick around. But now both of them wanted Ariel to be in their lives, to stay in their lives, to become a part of this island community for longer than one winter season.

Ariel glanced away from Hallie, and her gaze met with his. Her smile blossomed even more, causing his pulse to kick up a notch. He watched as she said something to Hallie and the other two women, then moved away from them and toward him, her passage unobstructed now that most of the congregation had left the sanctuary.

"Good morning," she said as she drew close.

"Morning."

"I was just asked to be part of the festival committee." She glanced over her shoulder. "Mrs. Harlowe wanted me to judge the short story entries."

He winced, guessing what she would say next.

Ariel met his gaze again. "I told them I couldn't because I'd already read the opening of one of the stories, and I would be biased."

"I'm sorry. I should've thought of that before I let

Shauna share her story with you. I should've known they would ask you to judge. You would've been a natural."

"It isn't your fault. Besides, being a novelist doesn't mean I'd be a good judge of children's writing. And it doesn't matter. They said they can put me to use else-where so it isn't a big deal."

"I suppose, since you won't be judging, you could go ahead and read Shauna's entry."

"She finished her story?"

He grinned. "Yes, and I've got to say, I think it's great."

"You wouldn't be biased, too, would you?"

"Of course I would. But I'm right, as well."

She laughed softly—and thoughts of kissing her returned.

"Shauna and I are going to eat at Eastside Cafe. Care to join us?"

She hesitated, a tiny frown furrowing her brow. He feared she was about to decline the invitation. Then her smile returned. "I haven't been there yet. I would love to join you."

They turned in unison and started toward the doorway to the narthex. Before they reached it, Shauna and Lily Morley came bursting through the opening.

"Dad!"

Before he could respond, she turned to Ariel.

"Hi, Miss Highbridge."

"Hi, yourself." Ariel's gaze shifted to the other little girl. "Hello, Lily."

"You remembered her name," Shauna said, beaming.

"How could I forget? I'm quite certain you and Lily

asked the most questions the day I visited your class. Didn't you?"

Shauna and Lily giggled with pleasure as they exchanged a look.

Sobering, Shauna turned her attention on her dad again. "Can Lily come with us to eat?"

"What's her mom say?"

"She says it's okay," Lily answered. "But I'm to go home right after and not bug you longer than necessary on a Sunday."

Tom laughed. "You won't bug me."

"She says you already spend school days with me and that's enough for anybody who isn't a member of the Morley family."

Tom laughed again, but before he could reply, Shauna took her friend's hand and drew Lily toward the doorway, calling out, "We'll wait for you outside, Dad."

"Best friends?" Ariel asked.

"Since they were five."

They followed after the girls.

"Is it hard? Knowing everyone so well. Teaching their kids. Having both your daughter and her best friend in your class for two years."

"It can be. Keeping the right balance is tricky at times. The island population is so small in the winter, we pretty much know everybody's business, whether we want to or not. But most of us figure it out."

"I've got neighbors in Boise who I've never met, let alone know anything about them. That's on me. I tend to isolate, especially when I'm writing."

Before they exited through the main doors, Ariel

stopped to zip up her coat, and Tom removed the knit cap from the pocket of his coat and pulled it onto his head. He held the door for her, and they stepped outside.

The sunlight reflecting off the snow was almost blinding, and both of them quickly slipped on sunglasses. Afterward, Tom offered his elbow. It pleased him that there was no hesitation on her part this time. She slid her hand into the crook of his arm, as if they'd been walking together that way for years.

"Hurry up, Dad. I'm starving."

Ariel laughed softly. "Is Shauna *always* hungry?"

"Seems like it. Luckily for me, she isn't hard to please. Whatever I put before her she'll eat."

"She seems more than a little excited to go to the Eastside Cafe."

"Eating out is a rare treat for us.

"What about the Shore View Palace? Have you ever eaten there?"

"Not with Shauna. I wanted to take Christina for our anniversary one year, but she forbid it because of the expense. She always knew how to hold us to our budget." He drew in a breath. "I wish I'd taken her anyway."

"I'm sorry. I shouldn't have asked."

"No. It's okay. The Palace really is expensive. It's not meant for the locals. It's for tourists." *Or*, he thought, *guys trying to impress a date.*

He imagined himself, Ariel by his side, in one of those horse drawn carriages the summer tourists loved. He could see it pulling up to the front entrance of the hotel on a balmy June evening, tiny white lights twinkling from bushes and trees. Delight would sparkle in her eyes as he escorted her into the main restaurant. Romantic music would fill the air and—

He clamped down on his fanciful thoughts. Once again, he was getting ahead of himself. But if Ariel did stay on in Sanctuary, if their relationship grew stronger, he would manage to find the money in his budget to take her there. So help him, he would.

ARIEL SENSED a change in Tom before their group of four reached the cafe. He didn't pull his arm away, didn't release her as they traversed the sidewalks. But she felt him withdraw emotionally. That hurt a little bit and made her worry that she'd said something wrong.

The girls opened the double glass doors, each of them on one side, and waved Tom and Ariel through.

"Hey, Tom," a pretty, dark-haired woman, who looked to be about Ariel's age, greeted him. "Hey, Shauna, Lily." The server's eyes settled on Ariel, inviting an introduction.

"Hi, Winona," Tom responded. "This is Ariel Highbridge, my . . . neighbor."

Ariel ignored the odd sting in her heart, a sting she didn't comprehend. She *was* his neighbor. What else should he call her? Only, it had begun to feel like there was more between them than mere location. At least it had felt that way up until a few minutes ago.

Winona grabbed a stack of plastic-covered menus. "Follow me." She led them toward a corner booth at the back of the building. "Will this do?"

"Yes," Shauna answered as she and Lily slid around to the far side. "It's *our* booth."

"That it is." Winona slid menus to the girls and to spots in front of the empty places on each side of them.

Tom motioned for Ariel to sit next to Lily, then he sat across from her, Shauna on his left.

"I'll be right back with some water," Winona said before walking away.

Ariel looked at Shauna. "What's good here?"

"Dad and I like their country-fried steak. Don't we, Dad?"

"We do."

"They've got really good hash browns, too. All the breakfast stuff is good, but Dad's are just as good so we skip those and go for something he never makes at home."

Ariel smiled as she turned her eyes to the menu. "Makes sense to me."

Conversations buzzed at other tables, but the four of them were silent as they decided what to order. Winona returned with glasses of water and set them on the table before pulling her order pad from a pocket.

Shauna didn't give the server a chance to ask what she wanted. She ordered the country-fried steak.

"As if I didn't know," Winona said, giving the girl a wink.

Ariel felt a strange desire to grind her teeth and was glad when the orders were taken and the server retreated once again.

"Mr. Fuller," Lily said, "are you helping with the tree lighting at the festival?"

"Sure am."

"Tree lighting?" Ariel looked at Tom. "But the tree in the square is already decorated."

"The big tree is. But we put lights on all the trees in the town square. We don't light them up until the Friday night before the festival."

Shauna leaned forward against the table. "The festival lasts all day on Saturday. There's a bunch of caroling. There's a Santa's grotto where the little kids get photos taken with him." She exchanged a look with Lily and lowered her voice. "We know who dresses up like Saint Nick every year, but we won't tell 'cause little kids don't know yet."

Ariel whispered, "Good for you."

"When it's cold enough and there's plenty of snow, there's snow sculpting. It's fun to watch. There's games to play and some races on skis and snowshoes. There's hot chocolate and cookies and crafts you can buy, if you want."

"And once it gets dark, there's fireworks," Lily chimed in.

"Sounds like a full day."

"It is," Tom said, "and it's fun for everyone."

"I'm looking forward to it." What she wanted to say was she looked forward to experiencing at least part of the day with Tom and Shauna. But the buzz of her phone caused her to look away. Steven Kipping's image stared back at her.

It had been over three weeks since Steven called with the news he meant to close his literary agency. The silence in the days since should have bothered her. Surprisingly, it hadn't. In fact, she was tempted to ignore the call now. But it was unusual for him to call on a Sunday. Finally, before it could go to voicemail, her curiosity got the better of her. She excused herself and swiped to accept the call.

"Hi, Steven."

"Ariel. Great. I was afraid I'd missed you."

"Didn't miss me, but give me a second." She held up an index finger toward Tom, indicating she wouldn't be long. Then she rose and walked toward the entrance to the cafe, hoping to find a quieter area. There didn't seem to be one. "I'm at a restaurant, Steven, and it's difficult to hear. May I call you back later?"

"Sure. That would be fine. Just wanted you to know I've got another agent willing to represent you. I'd like to tell you about him and get the two of you connected."

"Who is it?"

"Michael Prescott."

Ariel knew the name. One of her writer friends was repped by him. He was with a large agency in L.A., and he had a reputation for being somewhat of a shark. Would that be good for her or not? Would they work well together? And what would he think when she admitted she'd given herself a break from writing?

"Ariel? You there?"

"I'm here, Steven. Could I call you back at three o'clock?"

"Central?"

"No, we're in the Eastern time zone. Like you."

"Okay. I'll keep the decks clear for three o'clock. Talk to you then."

Taking the phone away from her ear, she clicked to end the call.

A panicked feeling wound its way around her heart, a sensation she hadn't felt in weeks.

God, what do You want for me? Please make it clear.

She slipped the phone into her pocket and returned to the table, determined not to think about writing and the possibility of a new agent until three o'clock.

CHAPTER 16

Late the next morning, Arial sat at the desk before the window overlooking the snow-covered backyard. Her laptop was closed before her, her fingernails tapping the lid.

Should I be doing this, God? What's the purpose? I'll write this next book. I'll fulfill my contract. But do I want to write anything after that? Do I even need an agent?

A look at the clock told her she didn't have time to consider those questions right now. After talking to Steven yesterday afternoon, she'd committed to meet with Michael Prescott via Zoom chat. There was no going back. She opened the laptop and waited for it to connect to the Wi-Fi. Then she clicked the link that had been sent to her. Moments later she was in the meeting room. Michael Prescott was there as well.

She'd known his name for a while and had heard of his reputation, but she'd never met him or seen him at a conference. After Steven's phone call, she'd looked at Michael's website. She'd expected a man in his fifties with salt and pepper hair and perhaps a goatee. That wasn't the man she'd seen on the website, and it wasn't the man in the Zoom room with her. The real Michael Prescott was a handsome, dark-haired fellow in his thirties. Not much older than Ariel herself.

"Hi, Ariel. It's a pleasure to meet you."

"You too, Mr. Prescott."

"No. It's Michael. Please."

"Michael," she echoed softly.

"Quite a surprise about Steven closing his agency."

"Yes, it was."

"But good for him. He's a man of integrity. His desire to serve the public is to be admired."

"Yes."

Couldn't she say something more intelligent than a simple yes or no?

"Listen, Ariel. I don't want to take too much of your time. Just wanted to get to know you a little and let you know me. I've looked at a couple of your books, and Steven's shared sales numbers and awards with me. I think I'm up-to-date on your past and current contracts as well. But what would you like me to know about you?"

"I'm not sure. May I ask something first?"

"Of course."

"I write Regency romances with a strong faith thread. Do you like that type of fiction?"

His smile was good humored. "It may not be the type of book I reach for on my nightstand, Ariel. But I assure you, I have respect for those who write them and those who read them, and I would be proud to represent you. If that's what you're asking."

"Did Steven tell you I'm taking a bit of a break from writing?"

"He did, and if it's what you need, I definitely support your decision. In fact, if you need it, I can talk to your publisher about an extension. I don't think it would be a problem at all."

Tension eased inside of her. "I shouldn't need an extension, but that's good to know in case I'm wrong. I'll have a better idea in January."

"Fair enough." He leaned back in his chair. "Now, tell me about this island you've retreated to."

"Sanctuary is like its name implies." She smiled as her gaze lifted to the scene beyond her window. "Completely charming. Right now everything is covered with snow. People get around on skis and snowmobiles, for the most part. Everything is decorated for Christmas. There aren't a lot of shops open in the off-season, so there isn't that usual feeling of needing to rush out and spend a fortune. I'm loving it."

Michael leaned closer to his computer. "Sounds like it was a good decision for you to go there. Give your brain permission to play without feeling the need to work."

She smiled and nodded.

"All right then. I'll let you go. You've got my email address and phone number. Send me the signed agency contract when you're ready. Contact me any time if you feel the need. Otherwise, I'll plan to connect with you in January."

"Thanks, Michael."

"Have a Merry Christmas."

"You too."

They said goodbye and ended the video call.

Before closing her laptop, she clicked open the agency contract Michael had sent earlier. It was a simple document, lacking an abundance of legalese. She appreciated that. And the exit clause was uncomplicated as well. It was a contract she could sign, despite how uncertain she felt about her future as a writer.

Yes.

The word in her heart seemed to come from someplace outside herself. She didn't know how else to describe it. Just a certainty this was a step she should take.

"God, I hope that's Your voice I hear. I hope that's the answer to all my prayers this past week. Stop me from signing if that yes isn't from You."

She closed the document, then reached for her iPad and opened the same document there. Pausing to take a breath, she listened for God's voice. The *Yes* still lingered in her heart. Taking up her electronic pencil, she signed the document. After saving it, she emailed it back to Michael Prescott.

WITH HIS STUDENTS busy with their reading assignment, Tom stared out the windows of his classroom, his thoughts on Ariel. How had she spent her day? She'd been distracted at the cafe yesterday after the call from her agent. A call from her former agent to talk to her about a possible new agent. That much she'd told him before they left the Eastside.

But to be honest, he had little idea what getting a new

agent meant, and the not knowing troubled him. He didn't want anything—or anyone—to pull Ariel away from him. Would a new agent do that? Would she start writing again and lock herself away in Gwyneth's house, with no time to spend with him? Or worse, would she leave Sanctuary and go back home to Idaho?

"You gotta kiss her, Dad."

When he'd dated his wife, they'd been in college. Still kids, although they hadn't realized it then. There'd been plenty of activities and distractions, plenty of places he could take Christina to woo and win her. While he loved Sanctuary Island, in the off-season there weren't a lot of places to go and things to do. He couldn't take Ariel to dinner at the Palace or to see a play performed at the outdoor amphitheater or for a picnic on the beach. There was no movie theater, no cycling around the island, no horseback riding, no spontaneous baseball games with other locals.

Still, he needed to do something more than take her to eat at the Eastside after church. Something more than make a snowman in the backyard that ended in a snow-ball fight.

"Mr. Fuller?"

He blinked away his thoughts and turned his attention on Lily Morley who now stood beside his desk. "Yes."

"I finished my reading. Can I work on my story for the festival? I gotta turn it in on Wednesday, and it's not done yet."

"Sure," he answered. "That will be fine. Just work quietly."

While Lily returned to her desk, Tom's gaze went to

his daughter, bent over her book, her brow furrowed and the tip of her tongue in the corner of her mouth as she concentrated.

Shauna had chosen not to share her finished story with Ariel, despite Ariel's willingness to read it. Shauna said she would rather wait until the contest was over. Yesterday afternoon, she had carefully copied the story from her journal onto lined paper, and this morning she'd dropped her entry into the festival's collection box in the school office. Of course, she hoped she would win the prize, and he hoped so too. He'd thought her story inventive and delightful.

"You wouldn't be biased, too, would you?"

The memory of Ariel's question made him smile again. He absolutely *was* biased. No question about it. But it seemed, so was Ariel. Didn't that bode well for his cause?

He would ask Ariel out on a date for this weekend. Dinner and a movie at his house on Saturday night. He would have Shauna do a sleepover at Lily's. He knew her parents would help him out that way. He would fix a really nice meal. Something special. Nothing like tuna casserole or spaghetti which were staples in the Fuller household. No, something more like grilled steaks and baked potatoes with all the fixings and a nice tossed green salad with cucumber and tomato slices. Hopefully his freezer and the Island Market would cooperate in his endeavor.

His TV wasn't huge but it seemed large in his living room. Turning the lights down low and making a fire in the fireplace would add ambience. He could ask Ariel about her favorite type of movie. Surely something good would be available for streaming.

The bell rang to dismiss students for lunch, startling Tom from his reverie. He felt guilty as he took in his students, all of them watching him expectantly. He'd better get better control of his thoughts. There was still plenty of the school day remaining.

As soon as he was alone in the classroom, he took out his phone and opened the message app.

TOM:

Enjoyed yesterday. Glad you came with us to eat at the Eastside. Was wondering if you would join me Saturday for dinner and movie.

. . .

ARIEL:

I enjoyed yesterday too. Dinner and a 🎥? Where?

TOM:

Fuller house. Menu calls for steak and baked potatoes. Not sure what vegetable. Movie selection depends upon streaming service offerings.

. . .

ARIEL:

What can I bring?

TOM:

Just yourself.

ARIEL:

Time?

TOM:

Dinner at 6 pm.

. . .

ARIEL:

I'll be there

TOM:

Favorite type films?

ARIEL:

Anything Jane Austen

TOM:

LOL! Of course. Should have known.

He grinned. That had been easier than expected. Painless even. What had he been worried about? It was obvious he and Ariel got along well. Of course, that didn't do away with the teeny-tiny problem of her home being a good fifteen hundred miles away from Sanctuary Island. But they could address that problem after they knew for certain they wanted a future together.

The only way they would know that was if they both fell unmistakably, irrevocably in love.

For the first time since his college days, he was willing to give that a try.

CHAPTER 17

A few mornings later, Ariel awakened with a start, a dream vivid in her memory. After a quick glance at the dimly-lit face of the digital clock, she stared toward the ceiling, her bedroom still pitch black at this hour in December.

In the way of dreams, hers had been about her dad but not really about her dad. She'd been a part of the story in her mind and yet had been watching it from a distance. Something deep in her heart told her this dream was something she should remember, should think about, perhaps should write about.

Should write about? She'd set aside all thoughts of writing until the end of the year to focus on deepening her relationship with Christ. Was this a temptation she should ignore? Or had God Himself sent the dream?

That thought made her pause. It had been a long while since she'd considered whether God was concerned about all the little details of her days. And yet the Bible told her that was true. If He knew how many hairs were on her head and when a single sparrow fell, as the Bible said, then surely He knew her dreams and what she should do with them.

She closed her eyes and replayed the dream, wanting to imprint it on her memory. Too often dreams came and were quickly forgotten. She didn't want this one to go that way.

Dad had looked strong and healthy in the dream, a familiar twinkle in his eyes when he'd looked her way. She'd felt both seen and loved, and she allowed herself to take pleasure in those feelings. Dad hadn't said anything in the dream, and yet she sensed he'd spoken to her, had wanted her to know something important.

Twelve years. It had been over twelve years since her dad died, suddenly, unexpectedly, crashing the security of Ariel's world. In a strange way, he'd become the first man to fail her. Not fair, of course, to feel that way as he hadn't chosen to have a heart attack in his mid-forties. All the same, by his death, Dad had abandoned her. She'd never actually considered that before. Why would she? It wasn't rational.

"Feelings are feelings," her mom liked to say. *"They aren't right or wrong. They just are. It's what you do with them that matters."*

"What I do with them," Ariel whispered.

She sat up, pushing aside the bedcovers. After putting on her slippers, she reached for her fluffy bathrobe and cinched the belt around her waist as she walked out of the room and down the short hall, pausing long enough to raise the heat control. By the time she sat at the desk, her laptop coming to life and two lamps dispelling shadows, she heard the furnace start to run, blowing heat through the floor vents and taking some of the winter chill from the living room.

She opened her writing application and wrote down the dream and the emotions it had stirred to life. The more she wrote, the more her feelings became clear and the more there seemed to be to write about.

It's going to be a novel.

Her fingers stilled. A novel? But that wasn't possible. She couldn't put these thoughts into a Regency romance. She saw it unfolding in the present day. And the ideas wouldn't translate well into the early 1800s in England. This was a contemporary story. An American story. Perhaps it was even a personal story.

She typed again, making bullet points of random thoughts as they came, like staccato notes on a piano.

Ariel was more of an intuitive writer than one who followed an outline. She always knew the opening of a novel, usually knew the ending, but often had no clear path how she wanted the story to reach that ending. She wrote to discover what would happen next, the same way her readers read to discover what would happen next.

But this morning was different. The more she put down her ideas, the clearer the story became in her mind. Secrets and betrayals. Joys and heartbreaks. A family broken and repaired. God's sovereignty and the valleys He would guide the characters through.

She couldn't seem to type fast enough.

FOR MORE THAN FORTY YEARS, a men's support group for widowers had met every first and third Thursday night at Sanctuary Bible Church. Thankfully, on this small island, they didn't have a steady influx of new members. Tom had found his way to the meetings within the first couple of months after Christina died. Three of the other men were over sixty, the eldest getting close to ninety. Tom was one of two men in the group who were still in their thirties.

Although he didn't need the same emotional support from these men that he once had and only attended occasionally, he valued them as his brothers in Christ. They not only encouraged him, but they held him accountable for the way he chose to live. Tom found great value in that, and so he continued to meet with these men when he could—as well as to pray they wouldn't add a new member any time soon because that meant heartbreak for someone.

"Hey, Tom," Ed Masters greeted him from a circle of six chairs, four still empty. "Good to see you here again. Been a couple of months."

"Hey, Ed." He went to a nearby table and poured water into a plastic cup. "How's business?"

"Quiet." Ed was an electrician who stayed *busy enough*, as he liked to put it, in the winter. Summers were much more demanding.

Henry Acorn, seated on the chair to Ed's left, ran a hand over the worn cover of the Bible on his lap. "And how's that girl of yours, Tom?"

For a split second, Tom thought Henry meant Ariel.

"Shauna told me at church that she's entering a story in the festival contest."

Tom released a breath, then smiled, relieved for a different subject. "Yes." He sat in a chair opposite Ed. "Her story's good, too."

"Not surprised," Henry said. "That girl has quite the imagination. She's a great kid, Tom. You've done a good job raising her."

"With God's help. And Christina gets a lot of the credit for starting her out right."

"Amen," Ed said before glancing at his watch, then toward the door. "Looks like it's just going to be the three of us tonight. Either of you have a topic you want to discuss?"

Henry answered, "I wouldn't mind talking over something the pastor said in his sermon on Sunday."

Without waiting for Ed to respond, Tom opened his Bible to James, chapter three.

"Pastor Keiser said something about how, in order to grow in true godly wisdom, we must first grow in our understanding of the God of the Bible." Henry looked at Ed, then Tom. "How do we increase our understanding of God's attributes? Is it only from spending time in our Bibles or are there other activities that contribute to growing in true understanding of God?"

Even with only three of them, Tom figured they were in for an interesting discussion.

NINETY MINUTES LATER, Tom headed west on Sixth Street, his mind replaying the evening's discussion. He felt challenged by Ed's and Henry's comments, questions, and suggestions. Challenged in the best sense of the word. He wanted to be a man who looked into the Bible and saw the beauty of God. He wanted to be a man who lived out true wisdom in his relationships with his daughter and with others beyond his own family.

An icy gust of wind almost brought him to a full stop. He leaned into it, head tipped forward, coat collar raised, hands tucked in his pockets. Another hot chocolate night with his daughter seemed in order.

He remembered Ariel seated across from him at the table in his kitchen as she and Shauna stirred hot chocolate with melting candy canes. He wished he could call and invite her over tonight, but they'd already made plans for Saturday. It probably was best not to push for more.

Of course, there was still the problem of location. His and hers. Michigan and Idaho. Midwest and Pacific Northwest. How soon would be too soon to bring that up with her? Moving wasn't truly an option for him. His life, his daughter's life, were here on the island. Their church, Shauna's school, his job. Shauna's memories of her mom were here. Her best friend was here on Sanctuary. Maybe he could move to another state and get a teaching position. But uprooting his daughter from everything she'd always known wouldn't be right. It would be selfish. Right?

Besides, Ariel had roots too. She'd always lived in Idaho. Her mom and stepdad lived there. She had a church and friends, a life apart that he'd never seen for himself. Maybe it wasn't something she wanted to give up either.

He leaned into the wind and started walking again.

I'd better put the matter in Your hands, Lord, and leave it there. Let Your will be done, not mine.

If ever wisdom was needed, it was when a man hoped to create a forever relationship with a woman, especially when there was a child in the mix.

CHAPTER 18

A riel held her breath as her finger hovered above the touchpad on her laptop. Then she tapped it, causing the cursor to click the Send key. The email *whooshed*, indicating it was on its way to Michael Prescott's inbox, along with the attachment of her proposed book.

She'd done nothing else for the past two days except write this proposal. She'd barely taken time to eat or sleep. Ideas had taken her imagination captive and spilled onto her laptop screen. Still, her stomach was a jumble of nerves and excitement mixed together because she'd dared to share it with someone else. Not simply someone else. With her new agent. An agent she had no real experience with.

How did Michael work? Did he read proposals or did he have an assistant read them first? Maybe the assistant read everything and then warned him if something wasn't very good. Was this proposal any good? She thought so but it was different from anything she'd written before.

Would Michael let her take a risk with a new genre or would he want her to stay in her own lane? She'd built a nice following in Regency romance. Would readers be willing to follow her into contemporary women's fiction?

She stared at the laptop screen. "Maybe I shouldn't have sent it."

Good idea or not, too much time had passed since she clicked Send. It was too late to call back the email with the attachment. It was out there now. Michael probably didn't work on the weekends, and traditional publishing shut down, for the most part, during the month of December. She might not get feedback from Michael until the new year. No point in worrying about it.

"I'll let it rest until next week. Then see if I still like it." Her voice echoed in the room.

After checking the time, she rose from the desk chair. She'd better hurry or she would be late for work. Cathy had told her they were introducing a new cupcake flavor today, but the older woman had kept the flavor a secret. "Something Christmasy," was all she'd been willing to say on Wednesday.

Ariel took a quick shower and, after blowing her hair dry, caught it in a ponytail high on her head. Since the kitchen at the bakery stayed quite warm thanks to the ovens, Ariel had learned to wear a simple T-shirt with jeans, then add a cardigan beneath her coat for the walk to and from the bakery.

She was on the stoop, locking the front door, when something bumped into the backs of her knees, giving her a start.

"Scruffy!" she heard Shauna call.

Laughing, Ariel reached down to pat the dog's head. "I should've known it was you." She turned around to see Shauna hurrying toward her, leash in hand.

"He was heeling pretty good until he saw you." Shauna snapped the leash to his collar. "Are you ever gonna learn?"

"It's okay. We're good friends. Aren't we, Scruffy?" She leaned low to pet the dog one more time.

"You going to Cathy's?"

"Yes. And we're introducing a new flavor today. Can't wait to find out what it is."

"Maybe Dad'll bring me by." The girl frowned. "Although he did say we wouldn't be getting more cupcakes until closer to Christmas."

"You never know. Sometimes dads change their minds."

"Sometimes," Shauna said, her tone doubtful.

Ariel went down the steps.

"Dad had me take Scruffy for a walk while he's cleaning house. He wants things looking nice for when you come over tonight."

Ariel's breath caught. She had a date tonight. A date with Tom Fuller. She'd completely forgotten. She'd forgotten anything and everything else after she'd started work on her proposal. But all of a sudden, those crazy nerves were whirling in her stomach for the second time, but now they had nothing to do with her writing.

"Is something wrong, Miss Highbridge? You look kinda funny."

"No." She shook her head and smiled as she started

down the walk. "Nothing's wrong. But I'd better get going. I don't want to be late to work."

"Okay. See you later."

Ariel stopped and looked over her shoulder, wondering all of a sudden if she'd misunderstood Tom's invitation. She tried to remember how Tom had worded his invitation. She'd have to look at his text again after Shauna left. Maybe this wasn't intended to be a real date. If Shauna was joining them for dinner and a movie, maybe this was just another good neighbor thing. "Are you having dinner with us, Shauna?"

The girl wrinkled her nose as she shook her head. "No. I'm going to spend the night with Lily. Dad wants to be with just you."

Ariel's heart fluttered. That answered that.

"Be sure and tell him what Cathy's new cupcake flavor is. Okay?"

Ariel waved. "Okay." Then she hurried down the sidewalk toward the center of town.

"Dad wants to be with just you."

Was that true? Had Tom actually told Shauna that he wanted it to be just the two of them.

Ariel stopped on the sidewalk and took her phone from her pocket, opening it to the text thread with Tom.

Was wondering if you would join me Saturday for dinner and movie.

There was no mistaking his words. That was a man asking a woman on a date.

"Dad wants to be with just you."

And that was a man apparently telling his daughter that he liked a woman in a special way. Ariel might not be the best judge of men when it came to romance in the 21st Century, but even she couldn't misunderstand that.

Do I like him in a special way too?

She looked at the buildings on both sides of the street as she walked. Quaint and full of character, especially with the Christmas decorations on the Victorian-style lampposts and in shop windows. And quiet. So very quiet, even on a Saturday. She liked it here.

Hadn't she been warned that winter—between the weather and no ferry service—could make some people feel claustrophobic? She didn't feel that way. But she'd only been on the island about five weeks. Would she feel the same after five months?

"I don't plan to stay that long," she whispered. "What does it matter?"

Even so, this little island was beginning to feel more and more like home.

TOM STOOD IN THE KITCHEN, checking for the umpteenth time that he had everything ready for this evening's dinner with Ariel.

The seasoned ribeyes were on the counter. The gas grill on the side patio was hot and awaiting the steaks. Potatoes were baking in the oven. The salad was staying cold in the refrigerator, along with a store-bought key lime pie he'd taken from the freezer. He considered key lime a summer dessert, but he remembered Ariel mentioning it was a favorite when they'd eaten at the Eastside.

Let's hope I don't burn the steaks.

He released a soft groan, then went into the living room. A wood fire crackled in the fireplace. All the flat surfaces had been dusted and throw pillows arranged and rearranged. A couple of cozy blankets were on the arms of the sofa, in case the room wasn't warm enough when they watched the movie. He had a few film options lined up for Ariel to choose from, based on the recommendations of Hallie Bastida. One was streaming for free on one of his services. The others could be rented for about four dollars.

He groaned again. The last time he'd been on a date, he'd been a dead-broke college student, but he'd still managed to spend more on Christina than four dollars and the cost of a couple of nice steaks cooked on a grill.

Would this night simply prove to Ariel that remote island living had its limitations?

The doorbell rang, causing his pulse to jump. He went to answer it, reminding himself he wasn't a college student any longer. He'd better not act like one.

Ariel stood on his front stoop, bundled against the cold and smiling brightly. "Hope I'm not too early," she said.

"You're right on time. Come in."

Once inside, Ariel shed her hat, coat, and gloves. Tom hung her coat on the tree near the door and left hat and gloves on the small entry table.

"I'm going to toss the steaks on the grill," Tom said. "How do you like yours cooked?"

"Medium well. Just a touch of pink."

"I think I can manage that. Why don't you go into the living room and make yourself comfortable."

"Is there anything I can do to help?"

"Not a thing. I've got it all under control." Was that a lie? He hoped not.

She hesitated a moment, then walked down the short hallway to the living room. "Everything looks pretty," she called over her shoulder. "Love your Christmas decorations."

"Thanks. Shauna's the expert with those." Tom went into the kitchen and picked up the plate with the steaks on it. He didn't bother with a coat before stepping outside and opening the grill.

DESPITE HIS NERVES and feeling out of practice in the romance department, Tom thought the evening went well.

The steaks were cooked to perfection, if he did say so himself, and the rest of the food seemed to please Ariel, too. Their conversation over the meal began a little stilted, unlike the other times they'd eaten together. But that didn't last long.

After the meal, they went into the living room again. Tom added more wood to the fireplace before sitting on the sofa with Ariel, leaving a comfortable distance between them. She was quick to choose the Emma Thompson version of *Sense and Sensibility*. Although it wasn't his normal choice of entertainment—he liked action movies, although these days he watched a lot more kid films than anything else—he was surprised to find he enjoyed it.

As the credits began to roll, Ariel pressed her hands together. Not quite a clap but almost. "Oh, I *love* that movie. There's only one better Austen adaptation in my opinion."

"Which one is that?"

"The Colin Firth BBC series of *Pride and Prejudice*. I was three years old when it was released."

"Wow. It's really old."

"Hey!" She gave him a playful punch in the arm.

"Sorry. Couldn't resist." The way she looked at him made something warm and luscious coil in his belly. "Want to watch something else?"

She glanced at the watch on her wrist. "To tell you the truth, I don't think I can stay awake for another one. I . . . I kind of burned the midnight oil the last two nights."

"What kept you up so late?" He switched off the television.

Her answer included a note of surprise. "Writing. A lot of writing."

"Really? But Ariel, that's great. I thought you weren't even trying to write for now."

"I wasn't. But Thursday morning I woke up and I'd had this dream. It was so vivid, and something about it demanded I write down everything I remembered. So I got up and opened a document. I jotted down everything I could think of about the story and the characters. The ideas just kept coming, and so I started to write actual scenes. Before I knew it, I had three chapters and then four. I don't know. It just feels . . . special . . . to me."

"I can see that." Despite the low lighting in the room, he saw color rise in her cheeks.

"Can you see it?" Her eyes widened.

"Yes," he answered, but now he wasn't sure he knew what they were talking about.

"I sent it to my agent this morning."

Oh, yeah. They were talking about her writing.

"It's different than anything I've written before. I'm not sure I can actually do it."

He leaned toward her. "Sure you can."

"How would you know?"

"Because I read one of your books. You've got talent."

She leaned toward him. "You never said anything."

"This is the first time I've seen you since I finished it."

"And you liked it?"

He reached out with his right hand and cupped the side of her face. "I did like it. It was . . . sweet." *Like you*, he wanted to add.

Maybe he did say the words aloud, because her eyes grew wider, then softened. The next thing he knew, they were close enough to each other for his lips to meet with hers. Sensations—both familiar and new—swirled through him, and he knew, if she chose not to stay in Sanctuary, it was already too late for him to protect his heart.

CHAPTER 19

When Ariel stepped out her front door the next morning on her way to church, she found Tom waiting on the sidewalk. Her heart did a little flipflop.

"I thought we could walk to church together." He stepped forward and lightly brushed her lips with his.

She thought of the kisses they'd shared last night and hoped she wasn't blushing. "That would be nice." She turned and locked the door. When she faced him again, she said, "No Shauna?"

"She's still at Lily's house. She'll meet us there."

They started walking.

Heavy snow had fallen overnight, blanketing Sanctuary in another layer of pristine white. The morning light reflected off the snowy surface, causing it to twinkle like stars in the heavens. The snowfall appeared unmarked by boots or skis. As if she and Tom were alone on the island.

Ariel tucked her gloved hands into her pockets. "Does Shauna spend the night with Lily often?"

"Not often. But enough. They take turns whose house."

"How long have they been friends? You told me but I forgot."

"Since kindergarten. Lily's parents moved to the island just before school started that year. She and Shauna met the first day of class and have been like two peas in a pod ever since."

They walked close enough that the sleeve of Ariel's puffy coat brushed against his sleeve every few steps. It made her wish she could tuck her arm through his. She pictured pressing the side of her head against his shoulder, could see herself laughing over something he said. An idyllic image. But she'd believed in idyllic situations, idyllic images, idyllic relationships in the past. It had only led to heartache. She didn't want to fall into that trap again. Tom was great. Sure. But this wasn't forever. She needed to remember that.

Didn't she?

She edged to the left, putting a little more space between them as they traversed the snow-covered sidewalk.

When they arrived at the church a short while later, they discovered fewer than usual had braved the wintery conditions. Many older members of the congregation were noticeably absent, Ariel supposed because they didn't want to risk a slip-and-fall on the new snow. She wondered how many of those who were absent didn't have family on the island, younger people able to bring them groceries or simply visit to help fill the silence in their homes when the weather was bad.

"Hey, Dad."

Ariel turned with Tom in time to see the church door closing behind Shauna and Lily.

"Hey, kiddo." Tom hugged his daughter and kissed the top of her head. "Glad you made it on time."

"Mrs. Morley made sure we were awake early."

Tom looked at Lily. "Did you girls have a good time last night?"

"Sure did."

Shauna grinned as she took in Ariel as well as her dad. "Yeah. What about you? Did *you* have a good time?"

The memory of Tom's lips on hers filled Ariel's head, and she quickly looked toward the sanctuary, trying to distract herself.

"We did," Tom answered. If he was bothered by the question, he didn't sound like it. "Steaks were cooked just right, and the movie was good too." Pulling Ariel closer in a one-armed hug, he added, "Right, Ariel?"

Was he announcing to Shauna, to Lily, to everyone else in sight, that they were a couple? Was she ready for that?

She forced herself to return her gaze to Shauna. "It was a very nice evening. We watched one of my favorite films, but it was new to your dad."

"Was it *romantic*?" Shauna sing-songed the word, a glint in her eye.

Ariel felt her cheeks warm because, once again, it wasn't the memory of the movie in her mind. "I think it is," she managed to answer.

"And you liked it, too, Dad?"

He chuckled. "I did. Honest."

"Good for you." Shauna turned to Lily. "Come on. We'll be late."

The girls took off in the direction of the children's classroom.

The doors opened again, and Rick and Hallie Bastida entered the narthex. The men exchanged handshakes and the women exchanged hugs. Then, as if they did the same every Sunday, they entered the sanctuary and walked to the Bastidas' usual pew. Rick led the way in, followed by Hallie, then Ariel, but Tom stopped one row back to speak to a man on the opposite side of the aisle.

"I heard you and Tom had a date last night," Hallie said in a soft voice the moment they were settled.

Ariel gaped at her. "You *heard*?"

"You must have told Cathy Schuller when you made cupcakes yesterday." Hallie shrugged and smiled. "She told Meg Humphrey when Meg was in the shop to buy some of those new peppermint mocha cupcakes." Hallie waggled her fingers at Meg, seated at the piano at the front of the church. "And by the way, I hear those new cupcakes are delicious. But anyway, Meg told me last night on the phone when we were discussing more plans for the festival."

Rick leaned forward to look at Ariel. "And after that Hallie told me." His grin was filled with mischief. "So how did it go?"

"We had a nice time, but don't go reading anything into it. Tom and I are friends. That's all."

"Friends is a good place to start," Rick said before leaning back against the pew.

As Ariel faced forward, she remembered Tom's kisses last night and his arm around her back, pulling her close, in the narthex. Would lightning strike her dead? Had she told a lie, sitting here in church? Were they *just* friends? It felt like more than that, even if she wasn't ready for it to be more.

WHILE ARIEL VISITED in the narthex with two other women after the service, Tom stood a few steps away from her, waiting for Shauna to join him. He wondered what Ariel's plans were for the afternoon. He would like to ask her to eat lunch with him and Shauna, but he'd sensed hesitation in her today. Something that hadn't been present last night. He thought they'd taken a big step forward in their relationship, but perhaps he was wrong.

"Hey, Tom."

He turned in the direction of Rick's voice.

"You know old Mr. Johnson. He's got that little place on the north side of the island."

"Sure. I know him."

"I heard he's got a problem with his roof. He woke up to snow in his living room. I'm headed out there to see what I can do to shore things up. Can you give me a hand?"

Tom glanced down at the jeans and boots he'd worn this morning. "Be glad to."

"Ride with us to our place. Shauna too. We'll get a bite to eat, then head over."

"Sounds good. Let me tell Ariel."

"Invite her along. She and Shauna can hang out with Hallie while you and I are gone. I don't have any idea how long we'll be, but if Ariel needs to go home before we're back, Hallie can take her."

"I'll see what she says." He stepped toward Ariel.

She looked away from the women she was talking to and smiled softly when she spotted him. Enough to make his heart flipflop, causing him to forget what he needed to say. He glanced behind him, caught sight of Rick talking to Hallie, and remembered.

"Rick's asked for my help with something. A home repair for a neighbor on the north side of the island. He thought you might like to go over to his house to keep Hallie company. Shauna will be there too. They've offered us all lunch."

She studied him with those pretty eyes of hers. "I'd like that," she answered at last.

He breathed out in relief. Maybe she wasn't as hesitant as he'd feared. "Great."

A short while later, they were all in Rick's truck, Tom, Shauna, and Ariel in the back of the crew cab and Rick and Hallie in front. With patches of black ice hiding under the new layer of snow, Rick kept his speed under twenty miles per hour, which afforded passengers on the right side of the pickup occasional glimpses of the lake.

"How far out does the lake freeze?" Ariel asked, leaning forward for a better view.

"Most years it freezes a few miles from shore," Rick answered. "Some years farther out than others. In a harsh winter, about ninety percent of the lake can freeze over."

"Wow."

"The most ice is usually in February and March," Tom added. "It can be thick enough to take snowmobiles over to the mainland."

Ariel turned from the window. "So the ice is just getting started."

Tom nodded. "The ferry's stopped running now because the ice forms first near the shore, both the mainland and the island, and that can spell trouble for the ferry. There are a few boats on the island with hulls that can break through the ice when it's like this. But in another four to six weeks, the lake will be covered with ice from here to Havensport. I have to say, it looks pretty when it's topped with snow, but it can be dangerous." He glanced at Shauna.

"I stay away from the ice, Dad. You don't have to worry about me."

Tom huffed out a breath. To at least some degree, he thought worrying about a kid was part of a parent's job description. Jesus told His disciples that worry wouldn't add a single hour to a life. Tom would go even further and say that worry definitely subtracted hours from a life. But try as he might to put all his cares into the hands of his Savior, he hadn't been able to stop worrying about Shauna. Not completely.

He raised his eyes and found Ariel observing him, a half-smile on her lips. And he was almost certain that what he saw in her eyes was, *You're a great dad.* Strange, how good that felt.

CHAPTER 20

Even though Ariel had spent Thanksgiving with the Bastidas, when she entered their home, she was awed all over again, as if seeing it for the first time. The beauty of the great room with its view of Lake Huron was almost more than she could take in. In addition, the fall decor had been replaced by even more Christmas decorations. She was tempted to sing a carol or two.

Rick and Tom took some leftovers from the refrigerator and prepared their own lunch so they could leave as quickly as possible. Ariel couldn't help noticing that Tom seemed to belong in this kitchen as much as he belonged in his own. She envied the two men their lengthy friendship. She'd had friends come in and out of her life. She'd lost track of the friends from elementary school, high school, and even many of her friends from college. Gwyneth Muldoon and Danni Graves were her only two constant friends. Since Danni lived in Boise, she saw her more often—although she hadn't been in touch with

Danni since the first week she arrived on the island. Gwyneth she saw only every few years if they were lucky. Was it her own fault that so many of her friendships had slipped away? The question made her frown. Perhaps she needed to figure that out while she was on the island. *And then do something about it.*

"See you later, hon."

Ariel's attention returned to the present just in time to see Rick kiss Hallie's cheek before he left the kitchen.

"Later," Tom called over his shoulder as he followed his friend.

Ariel wasn't sure if the word was for her, Shauna, or them both.

"Come on," Hallie said after the men disappeared from view. "Now we can eat. And we don't have to make do with leftovers."

"You're kind to include us." Ariel moved around the kitchen island. "What can I do to help?"

"I've got lettuce and cucumbers for a salad, if you wouldn't mind."

"Not at all." As she went to the fridge, she wondered if the lettuce would be as pathetic looking as what she'd seen at the market earlier in the week. But it wasn't.

As if hearing an unspoken question, Hallie said, "Rick and I went grocery shopping in Havensport yesterday. Just a quick flight, there and back." She stopped chopping a roasted chicken into bite-sized pieces. "Do you ever stop to consider what a miracle it is, that we can eat fresh lettuce in December when there is snow on the ground? The age we live in is filled with problems, I know. But it isn't all bad."

"Every good gift comes down from the Father of lights. I read that this week."

"James, chapter one," Hallie replied. "I think verse seventeen."

"Wow. If I hadn't just read it, I couldn't have said what book it was from. I still couldn't give you chapter and verse. I'm terrible at memorizing."

"I am too. But I make myself work at it a little each day. Hiding the Word in our hearts is so important."

"Miss Hallie," Shauna interrupted from the great room. "Is it okay if I watch a movie?"

"Sure. That's fine. But it won't be too long before we eat. You'll have to press pause when the food's ready."

"Okay. I will."

Ariel took a knife from the block and, after washing the cucumbers, cut them into thin slices. "Shauna and Tom know their way around your house."

"They're here a lot. Especially in the years since Christina died. We've got a regular group that comes for dinner once a month, but Tom and Shauna are over more often than that."

"What . . . what happened to Christina? Tom said it was sepsis, but I don't really understand what that is. Only that it's bad."

"None of us understood what it meant either until what happened to Christina. Sepsis causes a body to attack its own tissues and organs. Christina had a bout of pneumonia, and the infection spread to her bloodstream. No one expected something like that to happen in an otherwise healthy young woman. She certainly didn't know how ill she was, and by the time she did, it was too late to save her. Her death was very sudden." She shook her head slowly, her knife stilled in the air. "It was hard for everyone who knew her. We were all stunned. And things were very dark for Tom for quite a while."

Ariel looked down at the cucumbers, a lump forming in her throat.

"But his faith in God brought him through. And I have to say that you've been good for him."

Ariel looked up again. "Me?"

Hallie laughed. "Yes, you."

"I haven't done anything."

"You've done more than you know."

Ariel replayed the last five weeks in her head. Tom had brought cookies over that first night. A neighborly thing to do. They'd become better acquainted because of a dog that liked to dig under a fence. They'd talked over hot chocolate and cupcakes. Snowball fight. Speaking to his students at the school. Sometimes sitting together at church. Joining Hallie and Rick for Thanksgiving.

And there was that dinner and movie in his home last night.

Plus that first kiss. *Oh, that kiss.*

"Tom's happier." Hallie resumed chopping. "He's . . . he's more like the Tom we used to know. And that's because of your influence."

"Hallie, I—" She broke off, not sure what she wanted to say. That she was a failure in the romance department. That she'd had her heart broken once too often. That she had another life off the island. That she'd come to Sanctuary to write and that was all. "Hallie, Tom and I . . . We're neighbors. I like him but . . . But it isn't anything more than that. It can't be. It's impossible. I don't live here."

Hallie laid down the knife and placed the knuckles of both hands on her hips. "You say you like him. But when you look at him, it seems like more than that. God specializes in accomplishing impossible things. Maybe you should leave some room for Him to work out the kinks in the relationship."

"We don't *have* a relationship," Ariel replied in a stage whisper, her gaze darting toward the great room where Shauna watched a movie. The memory of that kiss rushed back to accuse her of lying once again. A kiss meant something. A kiss meant some kind of relationship. A kiss wasn't nothing, and she was lying when she tried to pretend otherwise.

Her expression softening, Hallie said, "Care to tell me what's holding you back? Because I think you feel more for Tom than you let on."

"Maybe some other time, Hallie. After I figure it out myself."

THE JOHNSON HOUSE sat on a bluff with a spectacular view of the lake. The view was every bit as beautiful as the one afforded the Bastidas in the great room of their home. But Isaac Johnson's house was decidedly different from the one Rick had built. No more than eight hundred square feet—a small living room, small kitchen, small bedroom, tiny bathroom—it was weathered and beaten and in need of more than a little TLC. Isaac's ancestors had never been among the wealthy people who'd settled on the island, but his lineage went back almost as far as the founding families. And his ten acres of land overlooking Lake Huron had to be worth a small fortune, even if his little house appeared ready to fall down.

The first thing Tom and Rick had done upon arriving was clear the accumulated snow off the roof. The next step was to cover the hole above the living room with a tarp and make certain it was secure against any strong winds that might blow through. After that, while Isaac watched from a frayed recliner, Tom and Rick cleaned the floor of melted snow and other debris that had fallen through the hole.

"As soon as the weather allows," Rick told the elderly man in a loud voice, "we'll come back and make permanent repairs."

Isaac cupped a hand behind his right ear, white tufts of hair sticking up in various directions. "I can't afford a new roof."

"Don't worry about it. I'll take care of everything."

"Don't like to take charity. What you've done is enough."

"Mr. Johnson." Rick leaned forward, one hand resting on the arm of the recliner. "Don't deny me the blessing of helping a neighbor."

Isaac's frown deepened. "Blessing?"

"That's right. I'm blessed when I serve others."

"Young fool," Isaac muttered before pressing his thin lips together.

When the work was finished at last, they bid the man a

good day and carried the last of the tools to Rick's pickup, placing them in the truck bed.

"That man needs lots more help than what we just did." Tom settled into the passenger seat and reached for the seatbelt. "I took a peek into his fridge when he wasn't looking. Not much more than a bottle of ketchup and a half loaf of bread."

Rick clicked his seatbelt into place. "I'll tell Hallie. She helps organize the food pantry. We'll put him on the list, whether he likes charity or not."

"He stopped arguing after you told him it was a blessing. Maybe Hallie can use the same tactic."

Rick laughed. "Then both my wife and I can be young fools." He pressed the button that started the truck's engine. "Speaking of food, I'm hungry. Those leftovers didn't last me long. What about you?"

"I could eat again."

Rick's grin remained aimed in Tom's direction for a moment more. Then he put the truck in gear and steered it along an ill-kept driveway.

Once the tires were firmly on the main road, Tom felt himself relax. He hadn't relished the thought of digging a truck out of a ditch.

"So tell me," Rick said, "how'd the date go? I'm guessing great. I mean, she came to church with you."

"It was good."

Rick laughed again. "I've got the feeling it was more than good."

"Look. Ariel's nice and I like her." He shrugged. "Maybe more than I should at this point. But I can't let myself pretend there aren't a million reasons that would keep us from making a go of it. Starting with, she doesn't live on the island—and hasn't suggested she *wants* to live here."

"I get that. But every relationship has issues. And face it, you wouldn't be the first Sanctuary native who found a bride who used to live off island. I could name a few unlikely romances that have happened this year."

"Bride? Buddy, put the brakes on. Ariel and I are nowhere close to using that language."

Rick's smile faded. "Maybe I'm wrong, but it seems to me a Christian who dates does so in the hopes of finding a lasting relationship. Right?"

"If that's true, maybe I shouldn't be dating at all. I'm not sure I'm ready for anything serious and lasting. And what about Shauna? I don't want her to get her hopes up and then be hurt."

Rick studied him for an uncomfortably long moment. "Tom, you're my friend. We've always been honest with each other, and I'm gonna be honest with you now. I don't know if Ariel is the woman for you. I don't know if God has another marriage in your future. But I do know the Lord wants you to live your life to the full. Don't stop living just because there might be some pain around the corner. If you like Ariel as much as I think you do, don't be afraid of what might happen if she doesn't feel the same. Take the risk and see what happens."

Up ahead, the Sanctuary lighthouse rose above treetops. Tom loved that lighthouse. It stood solid against the storms that could batter both the lighthouse and the rocky cliffs beneath it. Made him recall Jesus's parable about building a house upon the rock instead of on sandy soil. If Tom built his life upon *the* Rock—upon Jesus Himself—then he wouldn't be destroyed by whatever came his way. He might be shaken, as he had been after Christina died, but he would press on.

"We are afflicted in every way, but not crushed; perplexed, but not despairing; persecuted, but not forsaken; struck down, but not destroyed."

The words from Second Corinthians seemed to wind themselves around his chest. "Rick?"

"Yeah?"

"Thanks."

"No worries. No worries at all."

CHAPTER 21

Tom turned off the classroom lights and closed the door. Then he and Shauna made their way to the school entrance, the footsteps sounding loudly in the otherwise empty hallway.

"Hey, Dad."

"Yeah?" He pushed open the heavy door and felt a cold wind try to push him back into the school.

"Is it wrong to listen to two people talking if they know you're there? Is that the same as eavesdropping?"

He clutched his briefcase filled with papers close to his chest. "It's certain they know you are there, within hearing distance?"

"Yeah."

"Well, then I don't think I would call that eavesdropping. To eavesdrop is to secretly listen to a conversation. If people know you're there, it can't be a secret. Right?"

"I guess."

Tom looked both ways on the street, then he and Shauna started across.

"Why?" he asked when they reached the end of the crosswalk. "Did you hear something you think you weren't supposed to hear?" A number of possibilities ran through his mind. Mostly the type of conversations he didn't want to have to explain to his daughter until she was older.

"Sorta."

He looked down at Shauna and discovered her looking up at him. "Something I shouldn't hear either?"

"I don't know." She scrunched her face in that way of hers. "Maybe."

Would he be causing her to gossip if he encouraged her to tell him what she'd overheard? On the other hand, had she heard something that might bring her harm or harm someone else? If that was the case, he needed to know. Better to err on the side of caution.

"You know you can tell me anything, Peanut. And don't worry. I won't betray your confidence. This is just between us."

They continued in silence, the snow crunching beneath their feet.

"Miss Hallie thinks Miss Ariel's been good for you."

First surprised, then pleased, he tried not to show either reaction. "When did you stop calling her Miss Highbridge?"

"Yesterday. It sounded funny after I called Mrs. Bastida Miss Hallie."

"Yes, I suppose it does."

"But what about what Miss Hallie said. Is Miss Ariel good for you?"

Tom thought about the way he felt when he was with Ariel and answered, "Yes, I guess in some ways she is."

"Miss Hallie said you're happier than you've been in a long time. Are you?"

Silence, then, "I suppose so."

"And that's because of Miss Ariel too. Right?"

"Maybe."

"Well . . . I think you should let Miss Ariel know that. And that you like her a lot."

Hadn't he let her know that when he'd kissed her? He might be rusty in the romance department, but he was pretty sure a kiss was a dead giveaway.

"I think Miss Hallie wants Miss Ariel to stay in Sanctuary."

It sounded to Tom as if Rick and Hallie had conspired and wanted the same thing for him. And wasn't it exactly what he'd started to want for himself?

"Hey, Peanut."

His daughter looked up at him again, frowning against the sunlight. "Huh?"

"You understand, don't you, that Miss Ariel plans to go back to Idaho after the thaw? But Sanctuary is where our home is. This is where my job is. Miss Ariel's got a home —and a life—far from here."

Shauna stopped walking, forcing Tom to do the same.

"Dad, are you afraid of me getting hurt if she doesn't stay? Or are you afraid of *you* getting hurt?"

His daughter might only be eleven years old, but she was nobody's fool. Sometimes she was quicker to catch on than he was. "Both," he answered after a pause.

"We'll be okay." She reached out and took his hand. "Whatever happens."

Oddly enough, he believed her.

ONLY TWO DAYS had passed since Ariel sent her book proposal to Michael Prescott, but it seemed much longer, perhaps because of what had happened over the weekend. Her date with Tom. The kiss they'd shared. Her talk with Hallie after church.

I think you feel more for Tom than you let on.

Was Hallie right? Did she feel more? And why should she worry about it? That kiss could have been nothing more than the ending of a pleasant evening. Tom could be the type of guy who thought every date should end with a kiss. Except she was pretty sure he wasn't.

"I'm acting like a silly teenager. Good grief!"

She went to the kitchen and poured cold water from the fridge into a glass, then leaned her hip against the counter as she drank it all.

More exercise. That's what she needed. Too bad she didn't know anything about cross-country skiing or snowshoeing. Too bad Gwyneth didn't have a treadmill. That would be useful in the winter. How did people on the island who didn't ski or snowshoe stay in shape once the snow started to fall?

She returned to the living room and stared out the window at the backyard. Over the fence, she saw Scruffy darting in and out of view. A few moments later, Shauna appeared too. Shauna didn't have to think up ways to get exercise. She burned off a gazillion calories playing with her dog every day after school.

The ping of incoming email drew her gaze to the laptop. She awakened the screen and surprise quickened her pulse. At the top of her unopened emails was one from Michael Prescott. Knees weak, she sank onto the desk chair, drew in a deep breath and released it, then clicked to open his email.

Monday, December 9, 2024, 4:45 PM

Good afternoon, Ariel.

I've finished reading your proposal. I must say I was surprised by it. A very different story than I expected from you. But I'm excited. This has great potential. But it won't do for your current publisher. They aren't going in that particular direction. You'll have to fulfill your contract with something else. Something they're expecting from you. Another Regency romance.

But don't lose heart. I can sell this elsewhere. I'm sure of it. New York publishing is crying for stories like this one. In fact, I may be able to sell it to a movie producer even before I sell it to a publisher. That's how much I believe in it.

Don't expect any activity before the New Year. But I'm convinced you'll hear good news from me before the end of January.

Have a good Christmas.

Michael Prescott

General market? New York publishing? Movie producer?

She read the email through two more times, and it still didn't seem to make sense. She loved her proposal. She felt passionate about writing the story and knew it was different. But was it really *that* good? Or was her new agent exaggerating, trying to convince her he was doing his best for her? She was still just Ariel Highbridge from Idaho, the author of modestly-successful Regency romances. Sure, every author would love to see one of their books become a movie. Sure, every author would love to have an agent like Michael Prescott believe he could sell their work anywhere.

"What if I can't even write it? What if all I've got is a few chapters and some half-baked ideas?"

She got up from the chair again, panic making her heart race. Shauna looked toward Ariel's living room window at that same moment, saw her, grinned, and waved. Glad for a distraction, Ariel retrieved her coat, pulled on her snow boots, and hurried out onto the back porch. "How was school?" she called to the girl.

"Okay." Shauna took a few steps backward. "Wanna come over?"

Ariel glanced toward the neighboring house. "I don't want to be in the way."

"You'd never be in the way, Miss Ariel."

She wasn't so sure about that. But then, she wasn't so sure about anything at the moment. Not about her career. Not about her personal life. It all felt out of control. She didn't like it when things were out of control.

"I think you feel more for Tom than you let on."

"Come on," Shauna called. "You can play with Scruffy."

New York publishing is crying for stories like this one. In fact, I may be able to sell it to a movie producer even before I sell it to a publisher.

Her mind made up, she went down the steps, walked out of her backyard, and opened the gate to the Fuller backyard. Shauna waited for her, holding Scruffy by the collar until the gate closed again.

"Here." Shauna let go of the dog. "Catch." She tossed a bright orange Frisbee.

Ariel managed to catch it, much to her own surprise. A laugh escaped her before she steadied herself and gave the disc a toss, thankful it managed to soar through the air the way it was supposed to.

Scruffy bounded across the yard and leaped for the Frisbee while it was still aloft. When he landed, a cloud of snow rose all around him, obscuring him momentarily from view. A second later, he ran in Ariel's direction, the Frisbee clamped between his teeth.

"When was the last time you threw one of those?" Tom asked from behind her.

She sucked in a breath as she turned toward his voice. "A long time. Years and years."

"Doesn't show." He came down the steps of the back porch, pulling his collar up to shield his neck.

His smile caused a warm sensation to coil in her belly, replacing the panic she'd felt a short while before.

"Did you have a good day?" he asked.

She nodded, shook her head, shrugged.

He laughed. "I'm not sure what any of that meant."

"Neither am I," she admitted.

"Want to come inside and talk about it?"

Did she? She wasn't sure. Would talking improve anything? And if she did want to talk, it wasn't about anything Shauna should hear.

"Usually we save hot chocolate for after supper. It's our dessert most nights. But I think we could have it now, if you'd like." He held a hand toward her, as if waiting to take her arm.

"Say yes," Shauna encouraged.

"You'd drink hot chocolate morning, noon, and night if I'd let you," Tom told his daughter.

Shauna grinned before bolting up the steps.

"Say yes," Tom said close to Ariel's ear, his voice low and rich.

"Yes," she whispered, and followed him into the house.

CHAPTER 22

As Tom and Shauna prepared the hot chocolate, he said a silent prayer for Ariel, then added another for himself. Yesterday, when they were all at the Bastidas, things had seemed a little strained between them. He'd put that down to what Rick said on the drive from the Johnson place. But now he wasn't so sure. Not after what Shauna had told him on the walk home from school.

With candy canes melting fast in the hot chocolate, the three of them sat around the small kitchen table. Nobody said a word at first. Gazes darted from person to person, then back to the hot beverages before them.

"Hey, Dad."

"Hmm?"

"Can I take my hot chocolate to my bedroom? I'd like to do some writing."

"I don't know."

"I won't spill it. I promise. And I've got a coaster so it won't hurt my desk."

He took a breath, wondering if Shauna wanted to write in her journal or if she simply wanted the two adults in the room to be alone together. He suspected his daughter was engaging in a bit of matchmaking.

"Okay," he answered at last. "But be careful you don't spill. It's hot, and you don't want to get burned."

"D-a-a-a-d."

He smiled and nodded, then watched as she left the room, holding the mug carefully and staring at its brim.

"You're so good with her," Ariel said.

"I try to be."

"You succeed."

He met her gaze. "Want to tell me about your day?"

"It was . . . confusing?"

He chuckled. "You sound confused about whether confusing is the right word."

"Because I am. Confused."

"Did you get more writing done?"

"Some."

"Not as good as when you first got the idea?"

"I was thinking of . . . other things today more than the story."

Tom shook his head. Who was he kidding? He didn't know how the mind of a writer worked. He was more practical than creative. He could probably ask a hundred questions and not hit upon the right one.

He lifted his mug and blew across the surface of the steaming liquid, then put it to his lips and sipped. For the second time, a lengthy silence filled the room, broken only by the occasional sips of chocolate.

"You're a patient man," Ariel said at long last.

"Try to be."

"Have you ever wanted something, dreamed of something for a long, long time? A goal. A desire. Then when it looked like it might actually happen, it scared you to even think about it."

"Hmm. Can't think of anything off the top of my head."

Unless it's the idea of the two of us. His breath caught at the thought. *That scares me a bit.*

Thankful Ariel was looking down rather than at him, he lifted his mug and drank more of the swiftly-cooling chocolate. As the silence lengthened, he looked at her again. This time he found her gaze on him.

"Um… You have a bit of a mustache." A smile tugged at the corners of her mouth.

He chuckled as he reached for a napkin. "Cute on a kid. Not so much on a guy my age." He wiped his mouth.

"I thought it was cute."

"Ariel, what's going on between us?"

Her smile vanished. "I think we like each other."

"I think so too. What I'm not sure about is where it's going?"

A frown creased her forehead. "Do we have to know now?"

"Rick reminded me of something yesterday. He said when a Christian dates somebody, they should do it in the hopes of finding a lasting relationship."

Softly she asked, "And you agree with him?"

"Yeah, I think he's right. I'm not saying we have to decide anything right now. But it would be nice to have the same goal, in case this is what God has for us."

Ariel pushed the mug away. Did she want to push him away too?

"Tom?"

"Hmm?"

"Do *you* think God wants more for us? As a couple."

"I don't know." His answer was soft and low and laced with honesty.

"I'm ashamed to admit that, in the past, I didn't ask God who He might want me to date, let alone what might be the end result. My romantic history has been all about the feelings, the rush of emotions." She hesitated before adding, "Followed by heartbreak."

"I'm sorry, Ariel."

"When I was still having trouble writing my book even after I got to the island, I thought maybe I should spend more time reconnecting with the Lord. I decided it was my spiritual well that had gone dry, even more than my creative well. And I was right about that." She covered her face with her hands. "My priorities have been all wrong for too long."

"Surely not all wrong."

She lowered her hands and reached for her own napkin, using it to wipe tears from her cheeks. She sniffed. "I don't know why I'm crying. I'm making a fool of myself."

"Not at all."

She slid her chair back from the table. "I need to go home. I'm sorry. Please excuse me."

Tom stood at the same time she did. He had to fight the desire to take hold of her arm to keep her there. Instead, he watched her hurry from the kitchen. Moments later, he heard the opening and closing of the front door, and he sank down onto his chair again.

"I should've told her," he said aloud.

He *did* know where he wanted this to go. He did hope for a lasting relationship with Ariel Highbridge. This wasn't a casual friendship for him. His heart was already invested and wanted more, wanted a future. He should have told her that.

Was it what God wanted for them? He couldn't say for sure. But he hoped so. He really hoped so.

"You *did* make a fool of yourself," Ariel muttered as she sat on the sofa. "You shouldn't have gone over there."

It had been anxiety over Michael's email that had sent her outside. She'd loved the good news but even good news for her writing had left her uncertain about the future. She should have shared that with Tom. She should have talked about what this could mean for her career. How had they ended up talking about their relationship instead? Why had she told him about her past relationships?

"I spoke the truth, though. I haven't prayed about him and me. I've never prayed about the men in my life. Not really. Not seriously."

She looked toward the artificial Christmas tree, its lights twinkling, and a wave of loneliness washed over her.

"Father God. . ." she began, but no words followed. Her

mind was blank. Writer's block, even in her prayers. How pathetic.

She lay on her side on the sofa and drew her legs toward her chest. For a while, she continued to watch the twinkling lights on the tree, but eventually her eyelids closed and her thoughts drifted back in time. She could almost feel her dad stroking her hair as she lay with her head in his lap, crying over her first breakup with a boy. At sixteen, she'd thought her life was over because Greg Smothers liked another girl better. She'd been certain her heart would never mend.

"There's someone special out there for you," Dad had said in that gentle voice of his. "Your mom and I have prayed for that special someone almost from the minute you were born. We've prayed he'll be a good and kind man, that he'll walk closely with God and be guided by the Lord's wisdom and not the wisdom of men. We've prayed you won't be deceived by the words or outward appearances of others, and we've prayed you won't be deceived by your own heart."

But she hadn't wanted to know what he and Mom prayed for. She'd wanted Greg Smothers to call and say he was sorry and tell her she was still his girl.

The heart wants what the heart wants. Wasn't that what she heard people say all the time? Her heart had wanted Greg Smothers at sixteen. Last year, her heart had wanted Zach Miller. In between, there'd been others her heart had wanted. None of those relationships had lasted. None of her old boyfriends had become anything more than exes. Why?

What is it the Bible says about what the heart wants?

She sat up and reached for her phone. A quick search told her where she would find the passage niggling at her mind. In Jeremiah, the seventeenth chapter. Rather than read the verse on her phone, she picked up her Bible from the coffee table and turned the thin pages until she found it.

She read it aloud. "'The heart is more deceitful than all else and is desperately sick; Who can understand it?'" Then she read it again, silently this time.

"Oh, God," she whispered. "I have been deceived by my heart. Multiple times in my life. How do I prevent it from happening again?"

She pictured Tom in her mind, seated at his kitchen table, the tender expression on his face, the look of understanding in his eyes. He cared about her. He cared for her. But he also loved God and wanted to follow His will. Tom Fuller wanted to know what God wanted.

"So do I." She closed her eyes and pressed her Bible against her chest. "Lord, help me to listen to You. Not only about Tom or any other man You might intend for me. Not just about my writing, whatever direction that's to go. But about everything in my life. May You be first above all else."

The muddled, confused emotions, her unsettled thoughts, eased. Drawing a breath, she picked up her phone a second time.

ARIEL:

I'm sorry I left so suddenly. I didn't even say goodbye to Shauna. I hope I didn't hurt her feelings. Or yours.

TOM:

We're okay. Are you feeling better?

ARIEL:

A little. Thanks for being patient with me. I just need a little time.

TOM:

I understand. Let me know if I can help somehow.

...

ARIEL:

I will. I promise.

CHAPTER 23

While Ariel watched from the kitchen entrance, Levi flipped the sign on the front door of Cathy's Cupcakes from Open to Closed. As he faced her again, she breathed out a sigh of relief.

"What a day," she said. "I think every person on the island decided they needed cupcakes today."

"It was kinda crazy for a Wednesday."

"Kinda," she echoed.

From the kitchen, Cathy said, "It'll be even busier next week."

"How many extra tons of sugar do you think gets eaten in December compared to other months of the year?" Ariel slipped her apron over her head, then walked to hang it on its hook on the opposite wall.

"I have no idea."

"Oddly enough, I'm not even tempted to take any cupcakes home with me." Ariel removed the hairnet and stuffed it into the pocket of her apron. "That's a change."

"I got there myself a couple of months after I opened the shop. Good thing. I'd be about three times my current size if I hadn't. I'm already soft and squishy in all the wrong places."

Ariel reached for her coat. "I'd be doomed in a chocolate factory."

Cathy laughed.

"I'll see you Saturday."

"See you then, hon. And thanks. I appreciate you so much."

Ariel tossed a smile in Cathy's direction before exiting through the back door.

Rather than heading home, she walked a block south to the bookstore. She stopped before reaching the entrance when she saw that the window display of Whimsical Pages featured two of her novels in the midst of recent bestsellers. Twinkling white lights surrounded them all. Amused and touched, she proceeded into the store.

"Ah, there you are," Guy greeted her from behind the counter. "I was hoping I'd see you today."

"Why is that?"

"Because I got in that commentary you asked about a couple of weeks ago."

"You ordered it for me?"

"Sure. Don't want one of my good customers to have to wait." He patted the counter with one hand. "It's in the back. I'll get it."

"Thanks."

She watched him disappear down an aisle before walking over to the shelf that held lined journals. Yesterday, as she'd sat on the sofa with her Bible and a cup of coffee, she'd felt the need to write down her thoughts. For the most part, she was a digital-type gal. She loved texts and emails. Anything she could type or tap on her laptop or phone was good for her.

But there was something about writing private thoughts on paper, something about the right pen in her hand. She recalled reading Shauna's charming story in a yellow journal and pulled a matching one off the bookstore shelf.

"Yellow it is."

From the back of the store, Guy said, "I've got it here."

Ariel moved to a spot where she could watch the store owner's approach.

"Are you ready for Christmas?" he asked as he went behind the counter.

"Yes," she answered, although the truth was, there wasn't much to do to be ready. The few gifts she'd bought for new friends on the island had mostly been purchased in this very bookshop. *I have a one-track mind. Books.* She smiled to herself as she placed the yellow journal on top of the thick commentary. "That's everything today, Guy."

He'd started to enter her purchases in the register when her phone vibrated. She glanced at it, planning to ignore the call, but her mom's photo was on her screen. She whispered, "Excuse me," slid her credit card toward Guy, and moved away from the counter. "Hi, Mom," she said as soon as she was near the opposite wall.

"Hi, honey."

"What's up? I thought we were going to FaceTime on Friday."

"We will. But I missed you today so I thought I'd call. Doesn't hurt to talk twice in a week, does it?"

Something seemed off in her mom's voice. "Is something wrong?" And why had she called instead of FaceTimed?

"No. I'm just missing you, like I said. I think it's the season. You've never spent a Christmas away from me. It's hard knowing we won't see you this year."

Homesickness stung Ariel's heart, strong and unexpected. "I know." The words came out in a whisper, and she paused to clear the thick lump in her throat. "But we'll FaceTime on Christmas morning. Right?"

"Of course. It's on my calendar for first thing. Expect a call to wake you up."

"I'm two hours ahead of you here. You won't have to wake me up. The way you always had to wake me up to help with breakfast. Remember?"

Ariel's childhood memories of Christmas morning were filled with aunts, uncles, and cousins coming to the Highbridge house for breakfast—waffles with maple syrup and bacon and sausage links and cinnamon rolls. Hot chocolate for the kids. Coffee for the adults. Her mom had been in her element in those times. A smile had never left her lips as she moved from stovetop to waffle iron and back again. Nothing ever got burned. The waffles never stuck to the iron and were always the perfect shade of brown. Ariel had helped by carrying plates and platters to the table, but Christmas morning had been her mom's happy place. It still was.

"I'm sorry I can't come home this year," Ariel said, her voice tight again.

A sound—suspiciously like a sniffle—came through the speaker. Then her mom said, "I've been spoiled. I've had you with me every Christmas since you were born. Most parents aren't that lucky. Kids grow up and move far away. But you've always been able to be with me, even as an adult." She sniffed again, louder this time. "I'm being silly and sentimental."

"Mom, you're going to make me cry, and I'm in a bookstore right now. I don't want to cry when I pay for my books."

Mom laughed, and the laughter helped Ariel bring her own emotions under control.

"If you're in a bookstore," her mom said, "I'm surprised you took the call. I know how you are."

"It's your fault. You always had a book, and I wanted to be like you."

"But you got your wild imagination from your dad."

Ariel smiled wistfully. "Yes, I did."

"Okay. I'll let you go pay for your books. I love you, honey."

"Love you too, Mom."

"We'll still talk on Friday."

"Of course."

"Send me some more pictures of that cute little town."

"Sure. I'll snap a few on my walk home and shoot them to you as soon as I take off my coat and boots."

"I love you," her mom said again.

"Back atcha."

The phone went silent, and when she pulled it away from her ear, her mom's photo was gone from the screen. Homesickness washed over her a second time. She took a deep breath, waiting for the feeling to pass. Then she pasted on a smile as she turned to face Guy.

"Everything okay?" he asked.

Obviously, her smile hadn't fooled him. "It's fine." She lifted her hand, still holding the phone. "It was my mom. We're both feeling kind of sad, not to see each other for Christmas."

"Hey, you could always catch a flight over to the mainland."

She resisted a shudder. "I don't like to fly at any time, but I'm scared to death of little planes. I don't know why. I just am." She shook her head. "No, I'm on the island until the ferry runs again."

"Well. . ." His smile was kind and filled with understanding. "We're glad you're in Sanctuary. And I know you won't be alone for Christmas. Hallie Bastida would never let that happen."

Eyes misting, she accepted her card and the bag holding her purchases from Guy and left the store.

"You oughta call her, Dad."

Tom turned from the living room window to look at Shauna. She sat on the sofa, her yellow journal on her crossed legs, a red pen in her right hand.

"She needed some space," he answered.

"No, she doesn't. She needs to know you care about her."

He went to sit beside his daughter on the sofa, draping

an arm around her. "You know, kiddo, you need to let your dad handle this."

She squinted up at him. "I just don't want you to mess it up. You're kinda outta practice."

He laughed and hugged her close. What could he say to that? He couldn't deny it. He was out of practice. It wasn't even that he'd dated a lot of other women. He'd fallen in love in college, and ever since Christina's death, he hadn't been interested in dating, hadn't been tempted to fall in love again. Not until Ariel.

"Call her, Dad. You know you want to."

Yes, he definitely wanted to call her. But remembering her as she'd been two days ago caused him to resist the urge. Something was going on inside her. Something more than confusion about the two of them. She'd seemed to be wrestling with God. He knew what that was like. He'd done some wrestling with the Almighty himself. He hadn't come away with a limp, like Jacob in the Old Testament, but he'd found a greater faith on the other side of it. Better not to put himself in the way. Not now.

"Do you love her, Dad?"

He looked down at his daughter again and knew he needed to give her a straight answer. "I'm starting to."

"Me too."

"But that doesn't mean she feels the same way."

"I know."

"You'll still be okay if she doesn't stay?"

"I won't like it." She shrugged. "But I'll be okay."

"Good to know."

"Is it okay if I pray about it?"

The question made him feel happy despite his concern

for Ariel. "It's okay to pray about *anything*, Peanut. In fact, we should pray about everything."

"Wanna pray together? You and me. Now."

He smiled. "Sure."

Shauna took his left hand between both of hers and closed her eyes. Maybe he should have closed his eyes too, but he found it hard to look away.

"Jesus," she said in a near-whisper, "we really, really like Miss Ariel. We'd like her to stay in Sanctuary and maybe learn to love us. Dad says we should always want Your will for us more than we want our own way. But we're kinda hoping what we want is what You want for us. So if that's possible, could You make it happen? Amen."

Tom moved his right arm from around Shauna's shoulder and placed his hand on her head. "Amen, Lord. Your will be done on earth as it is in heaven."

Neither of them moved for a short while, but then Shauna looked up at him once more. "I still think you oughta call her."

"You remember what Grandpa Fuller calls you?"

"A pistol."

"That's right." He gave her hair a ruffle, then stood. "You're a pistol, Shauna Fuller. You're a pistol."

He started walking toward the kitchen. Time to start dinner.

Even if what he wanted to do was get his phone and call the woman he loved.

CHAPTER 24

On Friday afternoon, Ariel sat in the living room of her temporary home along with Hallie Bastida and two other women from the festival committee, Meg Harlowe and Vicky Williams.

Meg took a sip of the coffee in her cup, then looked at Ariel. "I know you decided not to judge the entries in the writing contest, Ariel, but we—" She glanced at Meg, then Hallie. "We hoped you would agree to present the award for the winning entry. Perhaps talk about the winning story a little. It would be extra special to have a real writer make the presentation."

Ariel's cheeks warmed with pleasure. "I would be thrilled and honored to do it."

"Oh, good!" Meg clapped her hands together. "I know it will mean a lot to all the kids who entered."

"When will the presentation be made?"

Hallie answered, "Early evening. Right before the fireworks start. It'll be dark by then and all the Christmas lights will be on around the town square."

"I'm looking forward to seeing it." Ariel leaned against the back of her chair. "I was surprised when Cathy told me she's only open two hours on the Saturday morning of the festival. So I'll get to enjoy all of the festivities."

"You should try your hand at the ice sculpting," Vicky said. "We've got plenty of snow this year. Although there could be a warming trend. But it's supposed to be cold for the festival and more snow is in the forecast."

Ariel offered a quick smile before bringing her coffee cup to her lips. She had no intention of trying her hand at sculpting anything. It sounded like a good way to embarrass herself. But she looked forward to watching others do it. Many times through the years she'd gone to McCall for the annual winter festival. The ice sculptures there were always amazing. True works of art.

"So," Hallie said, bringing everyone's attention back to her, "are there any other last minute items we need to address? We are eight days away from the event. It'll be here before we know it."

Ariel hadn't a clue what might need to be addressed. She was the newbie to all of this. But the other two women—pros after many years of organizing the event—both shook their heads.

"Then I guess this meeting is adjourned." Hallie reached over to touch Ariel's arm. "Thanks for hosting for us."

"I didn't do anything really."

"Sure you did. You welcomed us into your home. That's a blessing."

"Says the queen of hospitality," Ariel replied with a grin.

Hallie shook her head as she rose from her chair, the others doing the same. Ariel followed her guests to the front of the house where they put on their hats and coats, Vicky sharing the whole while about her sister who was spending the Christmas holidays in Greece.

After a flurry of goodbyes, the women were out the door and Ariel was alone once again. Silence swirled around her as she collected the coffee cups and carried them to the kitchen. She took the time to wash them, then put them in the rack to air dry. That task done, she returned to the living room and sat at the desk.

Her Bible lay open where she'd left it earlier to prepare for her guests. Now her gaze fell to the familiar chapter she'd read again that morning. Romans 8. A number of verses in that chapter had been highlighted, and she ran a finger over the first one.

Therefore there is now no condemnation at all for those who are in Christ Jesus.

Her eyes moved down the page.

And we know that God causes all things to work together for good to those who love God, to those who are called according to His purpose.

Her heart stirred as she read those words again, then her gaze moved down the page.

For I am convinced that neither death, nor life, nor angels, nor principalities, nor things present, nor things to come, nor powers, nor height, nor depth, nor any other created thing will be able to separate us from the love of God that is in Christ Jesus our Lord.

She leaned back in the chair and stared out the window without actually seeing anything. Instead her mind mulled the meaning of the words she'd high-lighted.

"All things work together for good for those who love God," she whispered.

Truly, could *all* things work together for good? Did that mean even being cheated on by Zach could work together for her good because she loved God? Yet when she was dating Zach, she hadn't really been following God as closely as she should. If she had been, maybe she would have recognized Zach's flaws and avoided the heartache her relationship with him had caused.

Immediately thoughts of Tom came to mind. Kind, wonderful, caring, handsome, and oh-so-kissable Tom. If Zach hadn't cheated on her and dumped her, maybe Ariel wouldn't have struggled with her writing. If she hadn't struggled with her writing, maybe Gwyneth wouldn't have offered Ariel this house on Sanctuary Island. If Ariel hadn't come to Sanctuary, she wouldn't have met Tom Fuller, a man who loved God and loved his daughter, a man who'd been faithful to his wife, a man who was a good neighbor and a good friend. Was it possible that even when she hadn't been faithful to follow God's leading as she should, He had still been looking out for her, lovingly guiding her steps, waiting for her to draw closer to Him? The possibility slayed her.

"Is that Your answer, Father? Is Tom the one You mean for me?" Her heart quickened, but she took a breath and waited. "Lord, if I'm completely honest, I *want* Tom to be the one. Please make it clear if You want that for me too. I've made enough mistakes. I don't want to make another."

The silence of the house seemed to wrap around her.

Not in a lonely way. In a comforting one. Peace warmed her heart.

Her phone vibrated on the desk. Was it time for her mom's call already? She lifted the phone and accepted the FaceTime call. "Hey, Mom."

"Hi, honey. How are you?"

"I'm good. You look good too."

Mom patted her hair with her free hand, a gesture that Ariel must have seen a thousand times in her life. "Thanks."

"Are you feeling better than on Wednesday when you called?"

The question seemed to take her mom by surprise. "Oh goodness. I hope you weren't worried about me just because I said I'm missing you."

"Not worried, exactly."

"Like I said before, I'm spoiled, and I know it." Her mom paused and smiled. "Ariel, you look so pretty. I think winter on an island agrees with you."

"I like it here."

Her mom's eyes narrowed and her brow furrowed. "What's up?"

"Up?"

"Honey, there's something about the way you look. Have you met someone special?" Her eyes widened. "Is it that neighbor you told me about? The one you were with at Thanksgiving. What's his name?"

While Ariel had shared most of what had happened in her weeks on the island, including how nice her neighbor was, she'd kept her budding feelings for Tom to herself. Perhaps because she'd been afraid nothing would come of them. Or perhaps because she'd been afraid something *would* come of them.

"I'm right. Aren't I?"

"Yes, Mom. His name is Tom. Tom Fuller. And yes, I like him. A lot."

"Oh, I'm so glad." Tears glittered in her mom's eyes. "I so want you to find somebody special. Somebody good enough for you. Somebody you can share your life with and grow old with."

Crying wasn't unusual for her mom. Patricia Sherman got emotional over commercials at Christmas. But despite that tendency, Ariel's concern returned. "Are you sure you're okay, Mom?"

"I am. I'm perfectly fine. Better than fine. And I want to know all about Tom." She blinked away the tears. "So you'd better tell me more."

~

TOM LEANED back in the chair behind his desk and breathed a sigh of relief. There was nothing quite like the last day of school before the Christmas break. It was difficult to make the kids think about math or reading when they knew the beginning of their holidays was mere hours or even minutes away.

"Dad." Shauna reappeared at the classroom door, Lily standing directly behind her. "Is it okay if I go over to Lily's for a while?"

"Is it okay with your mom?" he asked Lily.

"Yes." Lily peeked around Shauna's shoulder. "Mom's

baking cookies this afternoon and said me and Shauna can help her with the frosting when we get home."

"All right then." He looked at his daughter. "Home before dark."

"I know, Dad."

"I mean it."

"I will, Dad."

He smiled and motioned with his hand to send her off. Once the girls were gone, he rose and did some final straightening of the classroom. By the time he walked out into the hall, briefcase in hand, the school had fallen silent. Only the principal, Sandra Birch, was still in her office.

Pausing in her doorway, Tom said, "Don't stay too long."

"I won't."

"If I don't see you before, I'll see you at the festival."

"You know you will."

"Any chance you'll do the cross country race this year?"

She laughed. "Very funny, Mr. Fuller. My days of racing on skis have come and gone."

He grinned and continued out of the building.

The instant he reached the corner and could see down the next block to Gwyneth's house, his thoughts were all about Ariel. How was she? Was she still feeling confused? Had she prayed about the future? Had she thought about what he'd said? Had he been wrong not to call her when Shauna told him to?

Perhaps it was that last question that propelled him to her door. He hesitated on the front stoop, then knocked.

A single rap. Pause. A couple more raps. He waited, listening, and began to think she wasn't at home. Then a light switched on seconds before the door opened.

It would have been hard to describe what he felt when she smiled at him. A genuine smile.

"Tom." She took a step back, widening the opening. "Come in." She looked beyond him. "No Shauna?"

"She went to Lily's house. They're frosting cookies."

"I always loved doing that with my mom."

Once inside, he shucked off his coat, poking his knit cap into the sleeve before hanging the coat on the tree. Still on the welcome mat, he stomped his feet to make sure no snow remained on his boots.

"Would you like some coffee?" she asked, motioning toward the kitchen.

"No thanks."

"Well, come in and sit down then."

He followed her to the living room. "Hope I didn't interrupt anything. Were you writing?"

"No, I just finished FaceTiming with my mom. We're missing each other. The holidays. You know."

"Yes." He sat on the sofa. "I know."

Ariel took the nearby chair. "I've always been with her for Christmas or at least on Christmas Eve, even as an adult." She frowned. "It seems silly, but I'm worried about her."

"Maybe it isn't silly."

"Well, it isn't as if she's totally alone for Christmas. I'm not there, but she's got my stepdad, Wes, who's a great man, by the way, and one of Wes's sons and his family will be there too."

"Yeah, but you're her daughter. Her little girl, even if you've grown up. She's got lots of memories of you at Christmas. It's bound to make her nostalgic when she can't see you. And if this is the first time it's happened, it's got to be even worse."

"You understand perfectly."

He wished she'd sat on the sofa. He wished she was close enough that he could take hold of her hand. "I . . . uh . . . I haven't seen you for a few days. Not since Monday. I . . . I wondered if you're okay. You were upset when you left my house."

"I was upset." She smiled, so briefly he almost missed it. "But I wasn't upset with you. Just with myself. And I'm sorry. It wasn't right for me to just run out without explaining."

He nodded but kept silent.

"I guess I didn't know *how* to explain. I needed to think. And to pray." She took a breath and released it. "About us."

Tom's pulse jumped.

She met his gaze. "Tom, I like you. And I . . . I think maybe it could become something more. But there are complications."

"There usually are, aren't there?" He recalled a friend, earlier in the year, saying something about his new romance being complicated. But that had turned out well. Couldn't the same be true for Ariel and him? He thought it could be true. He hoped it could.

"There's my apartment in Boise. There's my mom. This island is so far away from her, and I hate flying. I mean I *hate* flying."

His heart rate picked up even more. Did she realize what she'd said? Obviously she'd given their budding relationship some serious thought. She was talking about living on the island, about the problem the distance from Idaho could create for her. That had to mean something. Didn't it?

"Not sure how many days of driving that would be," he said, "but it isn't an impossible distance."

She smiled again, but it lasted longer this time. "It's about fifteen hundred miles. I looked it up."

"So a couple of days if you had two drivers and were killing it on the interstate."

"Three days with reasonable stops."

"You're right. But it could be done in less, especially if you could drive day and night." He returned her smile. "Nice thing about being a teacher is, I've got most of the summer off. And I've always wanted to visit Idaho . . ."

"Tom . . ." She shook her head slowly.

"I'm not trying to rush things, Ariel. But I am saying the problems aren't insurmountable." He rose from the sofa and went to stand before her, holding out a hand. When she put her hand in his, his heart thumped wildly.

A moment later, she stood before him, looking up at him, a million questions in her aquamarine eyes. Questions he couldn't answer. Not completely. But perhaps he could make them feel less impossible.

With his hands gently cupping the sides of her face, he lowered his lips to meet hers. Although desire flared within, he kept his kiss tender and light, allowing his mouth to linger, aware that neither of them seemed to breathe.

When he drew back at last, he didn't go far. Only far enough that he could meet her gaze again. The questions remained in her eyes, but something else was there too. A longing that mirrored his own.

"Tom," she whispered.

"Ariel," he replied, his voice breaking.

When she said nothing more, he kissed her once again. And he knew, before he withdrew a second time, that he loved her truly, a love that would grow with time and nurturing, but it was true love even now.

God, let her stay. Make it happen, please.

CHAPTER 25

Ariel was thankful for another busy day at the bakery. It helped—although not one hundred percent—to distract her thoughts from Tom. Tom and those kisses. Tom and what he offered her. The potential for something real and lasting. With him. With him and Shauna.

Do I want to be so far from Mom? I love Idaho. I would miss the mountains. Do I want to live on an island? An island where I'm trapped every winter?

She hadn't minded living on Sanctuary so far. In the past six weeks, she hadn't once wished she could get off of it to do something she couldn't do right there. She hadn't felt deprived in any way living here. Even in the winter. Of course, falling for Tom might have something to do with that.

Falling for Tom.

Was it love she felt? If not, could it become love? Would it? She was afraid to think what might be or could be or would be. She'd been wrong before. She'd been hurt before.

God, how do I know Your will?

From the kitchen doorway, Levi called, "We're gonna need more of the peppermint mochas. They're going even faster than the regular peppermint used to."

Cathy answered, "Got more about to come out of the oven."

"Great." The young man disappeared from view.

One step ahead of Levi's request, Ariel was already preparing the peppermint vanilla frosting in a large mixing bowl. By the time she finished, the dark chocolate cupcakes were cooling on the worktable, and Cathy was crushing more peppermint sticks to use as a garnish on the frosting.

"These mocha cupcakes were a great addition to the menu," Ariel said as she stirred melted dark chocolate in a pan. "I don't think I asked before. Did you come up with the recipe on your own?"

"Yes and no. I tried a few recipes I found on the internet, then played with it a bit until I found what I liked the best."

Ariel wiped up spilled chocolate with a towel. "Well, I think they're perfect."

Cathy slid another batch of cupcakes into the oven, set the timer, then turned toward Ariel. "I don't suppose I could talk you into continuing to work for me after next April."

Surprise skittered through Ariel. "I wasn't planning to stay on the island come summer."

"But that could change. Right?"

"Gwyneth will return in June."

"She's got two bedrooms in her house."

"Three, actually, but she didn't invite me to move into one of them for good. I think she likes her privacy as much as I like mine."

Cathy laughed. "I didn't figure you would stay with Gwyneth forever. Just for a while." Her meaning clear, Cathy turned toward the oven again.

Delicious feelings rolled through Ariel. Identical feelings to the ones in reaction to Tom's lips exploring hers yesterday. A soft groan escaped, and she was thankful for the noises in the kitchen to help disguise the sound.

The people who lived on this island year round, people like Cathy, who made up the small winter population, truly did seem to know everything about everybody else's business. At least Cathy seemed to have figured out what was happening between Tom and Ariel. And people weren't shy about expressing their opinions either. Not Cathy. Not Rick. Not Hallie.

Was *that* something she wouldn't mind if she made this island her home? Or would she grow to hate everyone knowing every little thing that went on in her life? Of course, she wouldn't know the answer to those questions unless she allowed herself to stay and to love Tom and to become something more to him than the writer next door. Her stomach seemed to somersault, and she pressed a hand to her abdomen. "I *want* to stay."

"What's that, dear?"

Had she spoken out loud? She hadn't meant to. "Nothing, Cathy. Just talking to myself."

"Gracious, I do that all the time."

"So do I."

"I thought it was an old age thing. At home I talk to my cat. Don't know if that's less or more crazy." Cathy laughed again.

"I haven't owned a pet in years," Ariel admitted.

"Well, Scruffy's close to being your dog by this time. You've taken him enough pup-cakes anyway."

Tom and Shauna and Scruffy. Ariel smiled as she pictured them all together. And somehow, she felt as if she could slide right into that image in her mind and fit there. Like a family. The idea was beginning to feel more and more possible to her with every hour that passed.

IT HADN'T TAKEN much for Shauna to convince Tom they needed to stop by the cupcake shop after their visit to the hardware store. No arm twisting required. He wanted to see Ariel again. There were too many hours of the day when he couldn't see her. He wanted to change that.

"But remember, we're not buying any cupcakes," he told Shauna as they turned the corner onto East Fourth. "We're only stopping to see if we can walk Ariel home when she's finished with work. Right?"

Shauna gave an exaggerated sigh. "Right."

"Wednesday. That's when I said you could get another cupcake."

"I know."

"And Saturday's the festival. There'll be lots of different goodies then."

Shauna skipped a few steps. "I can't wait for that." She

was silent a heartbeat, then asked, "Do you think my story's got a chance to win?"

"Sure it does. But even if it doesn't win, that doesn't mean your story isn't great."

"How do you know?"

"You know what? You should ask Ariel. She's a writer. I'll bet she's had disappointments. You know, where she thought a book would win an award or hit a bestseller list, and then it didn't. But that doesn't mean the book wasn't good. There are lots of things we don't have control of in life, Peanut. Our job is to do the best we can with the work set before us. What happens after that isn't something we control. We leave it to God. Understand?"

"Sure, Dad," she answered.

Did she understand or did she merely want him to stop talking? He grinned, not caring which it was. One thing he'd come to believe about parenting. He would never be perfect. His advice wouldn't be right every time. He needed to listen to his own counsel and do the best he could, hoping he provided Shauna with the tools to make good decisions, and then he would trust God with his daughter.

Shauna hurried ahead of him and opened the shop door. Tom quickened his steps to catch up with her. By the time he was inside and closing the door behind him, Shauna already had her nose close to the display case.

Levi, the young man behind the counter—and a former student of Tom's—gave him a nod, then went to the kitchen doorway and said, "Ariel, you've got a couple of customers."

"What?" came her muted answer. Moments later, she

appeared. When she saw him, a smile curved her beautiful mouth in the most inviting way. "I didn't expect to see you here."

"We're not customers today," he answered. "Just your escort home if you want one."

"I want one."

The swift answer sent pleasure through him.

"Let me finish up something in the kitchen. Then I'll be right out."

"Dad?"

"Hmm?" He looked at Shauna.

"Can we get pup-cakes for Scruffy?"

Tom chuckled. "No. He's had too much of a good thing in the last couple of months, just like we have."

"He's gonna be awful disappointed. He'll sniff us and know we were in the shop."

"Life is like that sometimes, kiddo. Scruffy will have to get over it. Same as you."

The look Shauna sent his way made him laugh louder.

It wasn't long before Ariel came out of the kitchen, this time wearing her puffy winter coat instead of her apron. He loved the way she looked in that coat. But then, he thought her adorable no matter what she wore.

It's official. I've gone round the bend.

Shauna moved away from the display case and opened the door for Ariel to go through first.

"Thank you, Shauna."

His daughter motioned for him to follow Ariel, and he was quick to oblige, pausing along with Ariel on the sidewalk outside the shop.

"Need to stop anywhere on the way home?" he asked her.

"No." She turned north. "I'm good."

More than good, I'd say.

They'd gone no more than half a block when Ariel said, "Shauna, what do you like about Sanctuary in the summer?"

"No school," came the quick reply.

Ariel laughed, a sound Tom loved more each time he heard it.

"No, I meant what do you love to do in the summer."

Shauna turned to walk backward, looking at Ariel, her face scrunched in that thoughtful way of hers. "Dad and I go on hikes with Scruffy. Sometimes in the park. Sometimes we follow paths that take us all the way around the island. Grandpa Fuller calls it a good stretch of the legs. Oh, last summer I took some riding lessons. That was cool."

"Riding? Do you mean on horses?"

"Yeah. It was fun. And we go to the beach a lot. I'm a good swimmer. Aren't I, Dad?"

He answered, "Yes, you are."

"Dad's always got projects to do around the house in the summer. Painting and repairs and stuff like that. Sometimes I help him, but lots of times that's when I go play with Lily and some of our other friends." She faced forward again, seconds before Tom would have warned her they were coming to the cross street.

"I know you love to read," Ariel said. "Do you read a lot in the summer or mostly in the winter?"

"Summer too. We go to the library sometimes. But

mostly I get ebooks from a library where my grandparents live. We've got library cards, and I can download books onto my iPad to read." Shauna looked over her shoulder. "For my birthday, Dad bought me the Chronicles of Narnia books so I can read them over and over. Paperbacks with really cool covers. They're my favorites."

"I could tell that from the opening of the story you wrote."

That caused Shauna to turn and walk backwards again. "Do you think my story could win the contest?" She didn't wait for Ariel to answer. "Dad said even if it doesn't win that it doesn't mean it isn't any good. And he said I should ask you how you know if a story is good, even if it doesn't win awards and stuff."

"He said all that, did he?"

Tom turned his head to find Ariel watching him with a gentle smile.

"Yeah, he did," Shauna answered.

Ariel's hand entwined with his. "Your dad's a very intelligent man, Shauna Fuller. Don't let anybody tell you different."

CHAPTER 26

F ollowing the Sunday service, Tom stepped outside and felt a *splat* of melting snow hit his head.

"Just what we didn't need," Rick said, stopping beside him. "A December thaw."

"If it keeps up, there won't be any ice sculpting during the festival. Might not even be any cross country ski races."

Rick checked his phone. "It's supposed to turn cold again by Tuesday, and it looks like they're predicting more snow will come during the week too."

"God willing." Another drop hit Tom's head, and he took a step backward, away from the eaves.

"Want to come to our place for lunch? You'd be welcome."

"Thanks, but I promised Shauna a meal of spaghetti and garlic bread today. You and Hallie could join us, you know."

"Will Ariel be there?"

He nodded.

"Thought so." Rick grinned. "I think we'll leave you two to enjoy the afternoon without any tagalongs."

What could he say to that? He enjoyed spending time with Rick and Hallie, but today he preferred the idea of an afternoon at his house with Ariel and Shauna. Like a family, the three of them. Time for him to get to know even more about Ariel. Time for her to get to know even more about him. More time for them both to learn what the future could be like.

"From the look of you, Tom, I'm guessing you're in a whole different place from a week ago."

He considered Rick's comment, then nodded and grinned. "Yeah. I am. Things have . . . become clearer. For both of us, I think."

"I have a good feeling about the two of you."

Tom glanced behind him as more people exited the church. "I do too. But it's still the early days. Things could change. You never know what life'll throw your way."

Shauna came out through the front doors then, followed by Hallie and Ariel. They exchanged goodbyes before Rick and Hallie walked toward the parking lot on the east side of town and Tom, Ariel, and Shauna turned west. About a block away from the church, with no other members of the congregation nearby, Tom reached for Ariel's hand. Like yesterday, it felt right and natural.

"Miss Ariel," Shauna said, "you're gonna love the spaghetti sauce we use. Grandma Fuller and Dad make a bunch of it when Grandma and Grandpa come stay, and Dad freezes it for us to use the rest of the year. It's really thick and—" She broke off, glancing at Tom over her shoulder. "What is it you call it, Dad?"

"Tangy."

"Yeah, that's the word. Thick and tangy."

"I can't wait." Ariel squeezed Tom's hand.

His voice low, Tom said, "Maybe you can help make a batch this summer when my mom and dad come to visit." His heart pounded in his ears, and the wait for her reply seemed endless. Because she had to know what he meant by that invitation.

"I'd like that," she replied at last.

"Great." His heart continued to thump. Loud enough he wondered if she heard it. "We'll count on it then."

When they reached home, Shauna took Scruffy out to the backyard to play for a while, and Tom and Ariel went to the kitchen to begin preparing their Sunday dinner. As they moved from counter to stovetop to refrigerator— moving as if they'd done this together a hundred times— they occasionally paused to brush lips in passing. That too seemed like they'd done it a hundred times.

I love you. That's what he wanted to say right after he kissed her. Each time he kissed her. *I love you.* But not wanting to rush her, wanting her to be as sure as he was before he said it, he swallowed the words back, hoping she would understand in other ways. In ways that would make her want to remain on Sanctuary Island even more. In ways that would make her want to stay with him forever.

～

Was the kitchen getting hotter because the oven and stovetop were in use? Or did Ariel feel hot all over because of the crazy emotions rushing through her? If Tom kissed her one more time, she thought she would melt into a puddle at his feet, like chocolate in a sauce pan at the bakery. She might have found out if Shauna hadn't chosen that moment to burst through the back door, Scruffy in her arms.

"Can you get me a towel, Dad. Scruffy needs dried off before he can run around the house."

"Coming, kiddo." Tom tossed a grin in Ariel's direction before disappearing into the laundry room.

Humming happily, Ariel went to the stove to give the noodles a stir, the water gently boiling. Then she moved to the spaghetti sauce in the pan next to it and gave it a stir too, causing a savory aroma to rise to her nostrils. The spoon was still twirling inside the sauce pan when she realized what song she hummed. A favorite of her mom's, George Strait's "I Cross My Heart." Her cheeks warmed as the lyrics played through her mind. They expressed what she wished she could say to Tom. They expressed what she wished he would say to her. They promised a forever kind of love, and that was what she wanted—and thought she might have found.

As Tom returned to the kitchen, he glanced over his shoulder at his daughter. "Go wash up. Then set the table."

"Sure, Dad." As fast as she'd entered the room, Shauna was gone.

The timer went off, and Tom put on oven mitts before taking a baking sheet from the oven, the hot garlic bread, wrapped in foil, in the center of it.

Ariel's stomach growled in response to the odors wafting through the kitchen. "All of a sudden, I'm starving. What else needs done?"

Before Tom could answer, Ariel's phone vibrated in the pocket of her Levi's. She was surprised to see her stepdad's face on the screen. She couldn't remember the last time Wes had called her. She swiped to accept the call. "Hi, Wes." Phone to her ear, she walked out of the kitchen and into the living room where she could hear better.

"Ariel, it's your mom."

Her heart skipped a beat. "What about Mom?"

"She doesn't know I'm calling you."

"What is it, Wes?"

"She got some bad news last week. I told her to tell you when the two of you talked, but I know she didn't."

Ariel's hand, the one holding the phone, shook. "Tell me what?"

"Your mom went for her annual mammogram a few weeks ago, and they found something suspicious. So she had to go in for additional screening because they suspected it could be cancer, so last week she had a biopsy. She thinks she'll get the results in a few days."

Cold inched through her veins, and Ariel dropped onto the nearest chair. Cancer? Her mom?

"She said she didn't want to make you worry, but I thought you should know."

"Of course I should know."

"I wish you were here," Wes said, so softly she barely heard him. "I . . . I feel like I'm not giving her what she needs. I want to support her, but I don't know what to say.

It's hard. Your grandmother. Your great aunt. You know that's weighing on her, even though she tries not to let it."

"I know. I should be there."

"Should I tell her I called you?"

"No. Not yet. I need . . . I need to think what to do."

"I'm sorry, Ariel. I hate to tell you this when you're so far away. And right before Christmas too. But I didn't think it was right to leave you in the dark."

"You did the right thing, Wes. Really. I . . . I'll call you back. And Wes?"

"Yeah?"

"Mom loves you. If she's mad because you told me, she'll get over it."

"I know."

"I love you too."

"Thanks. Love you back."

The phone went silent, and she knew her stepdad had ended the call even before she lowered it from her ear. Only then did she notice Tom standing in the hallway.

"What is it?" he asked, concern in his eyes.

"My mom. They think she might have cancer."

"Cancer?"

"Breast cancer." She clasped her hands, as if in prayer. "My grandmother and her sister, Great Aunt Margie, both died of breast cancer."

"Oh, Ariel." Tom strode quickly to her, drew her up from the chair, and enfolded her in his arms. "I'm sorry."

"I need to be with her. I'm so far away and I need to be with her."

He kissed the top of her head before pressing his cheek against the same spot.

Tears fell and were absorbed by his shirt. "What am I doing here? I need to be with her."

"Then you'd better plan your trip."

She drew back, looking up at him. "How? The ferry isn't running."

"Rick can fly you to the Grand Rapids airport in his plane. From there you can catch a flight to Boise."

Ariel shuddered, and her knees weakened. "I can't. Small planes terrify me. I just . . . I just can't."

"Okay." He frowned in thought. "It's warmed up out there. I know a guy with a boat that can get through ice when it isn't too thick, and the lake's not frozen hard yet. Long way to go for that. We can get you to the mainland. I'm sure of it. Let me give him a call. You get online and check on Boise flights from Grand Rapids." He took a step away from her, taking his warmth and strength with him. "It'll be okay, Ariel. You'll see."

"Tom. . ."

"Don't worry about anything else. We'll get you to your mom. You'll see."

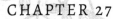

CHAPTER 27

The next day, after a somewhat unnerving boat trip to Havensport on the mainland, the iron hull of the vessel chopping through the thin layer of ice they encountered closer to shore, followed by a four hour drive to Grand Rapids—most of it made in silence while Ariel's thoughts raced—she stood in line to go through airport security, her heart thudding in her chest, her phone open to her boarding pass.

"It'll be okay, Ariel. You'll see."

Tom had spoken those words to her yesterday. He'd said them again as he bid her goodbye outside the terminal, the borrowed pickup truck idling in the unloading zone. Oh, how she wanted to believe him, both then and now. How she wanted everything to be all right.

"And we know that God causes all things to work together for good to those who love God . . ."

O Father, please work this together for my mom's good. Please. She loves You. Please work it out for her good. Please.

Her mom might have cancer. Her mom had had a

regular mammogram and then a special screening of some kind and then a biopsy. And now her mom might find out she had cancer anyway. Despite the precautions she'd taken. Like her mother and aunt before her. Like the women in the family who'd died from it.

Please get me there in time. Don't make her go through this without me. Please, God. Please.

She closed her eyes and remembered Tom's hug outside the airport. The warmth and strength of his embrace. She longed to still be in his arms.

"Ma'am?"

She opened her eyes to find the agent watching her. "Sorry." She scurried forward and handed him her license, then held her phone over the scanner. The remainder of her journey through the TSA line passed in a kind of blur.

A short while later, seated in the gate area, waiting for her flight to begin boarding, she called her stepdad. "Hi, Wes. I'm calling from the airport. I got here in plenty of time. The board says my flight will depart on time. I'll text you from Denver if there's any kind of delay there. If you don't hear from me, you'll know my flight's on time."

"Are you sure I shouldn't tell your mom you're coming?"

"No. Let's let it be a surprise. We'll call it a Christmas surprise." Her voice broke, and she had to swallow hard to keep back a sob.

"You know it could be just that," Wes said.

Could it? She wanted to believe that so much.

"It'll be okay, Ariel. You'll see."

"You still there, Ariel?"

"I'm here. But it looks like they're about to open the gate to start boarding. I'd better go. See you soon."

"See you soon."

As soon as she boarded, thankful she'd been able to get a seat at the last minute, she put in her earbuds and selected her favorite worship playlist in her music app, hoping to find peace in the lyrics. Her right leg began to bounce, and she placed her hand on her knee to force it to stop. It wouldn't stay still for long, of course. It was one of the ways her anxiety when flying revealed itself. Drawing a deep breath and releasing it, she selected the Photos icon on her phone screen. Tom, Shauna, and her own image smiled back at her. Hallie had taken the photo a couple of Sundays ago, then shared it with both Tom and Ariel.

"How soon will you be back, Miss Ariel?"

"I don't know, Shauna."

"You've gotta be here for the festival. You've just gotta. I've got all kinds of stuff I wanted to do with you."

"And I want to do them with you."

"Dad and I are praying for your mom."

"Thank you."

She touched her finger to the screen, lightly tracing over Tom's face, then Shauna's. They were dear to her. No, even more than that. She loved them. Loved them both. She wanted—

She broke off the unfinished thought as tears welled. Now wasn't the time to think about herself and what she wanted. Now she had to think about her mom, about what could be ahead of them. What would that be? Weeks and months of chemo? Surgery? Radiation? Medication?

She remembered her grandmother near the end of her life. Grandma Dot had gone through all the treatments, just as her sister Margie had done before her. Her spirits had been good. Her faith in the Lord had been strong. But the cancer had spread despite the doctors' best efforts and the prayers of the faithful, and eventually it had taken her. Grandma Dot had been buried between her husband and sister in a Boise cemetery.

The flight attendant announced the cabin door was closed. While the attendant began her usual instructions, Ariel checked to make sure her phone was in airplane mode, then turned up the volume of her music, trying not to think about take-off. Take-offs and landings, she'd heard, were the most dangerous times of a flight. But it was good to remember that thousands of planes took off and landed all day and all night long. She'd already prayed the pilots would be well rested and free of drugs and alcohol. Something she never failed to pray when she was forced to fly. Now all she could do was trust.

Both of her legs began to bounce. She pressed the palms of her hands against her knees. *Stop it. Stop it. Stop it.*

One flight of just over three hours.

A one hour layover.

Another flight just over two hours.

And then she would be home again.

So why did it feel as if she were flying away from home instead of flying to it?

∼

"Do you think she'll call, Dad, when she gets there?" Shauna hugged Tom around the waist.

"I don't know, sweetheart. I hope so. Or maybe she'll send a text message."

"Will she come back to Sanctuary?"

A heavy weight pressed on his chest. "I don't know. I hope so. I think it all depends on how her mom is doing." His gaze went to Rick and Hallie, who stood in the entry near the front door. "Thanks for keeping Shauna today. You didn't have to bring her back tonight, but I appreciate it."

"We knew you'd be exhausted." Rick put his arm around Hallie's shoulders. "And we didn't think you should be here alone. Glad to do whatever we could."

It had been a hard and exhausting day. More emotionally exhausting than physically, although the latter too. Throughout the drive to the Grand Rapids airport, Ariel had been silent. When he'd glanced at her, he'd seen how hard she fought to hold herself together, and so he'd said little to her. A few times, he'd asked if she needed to stop to get something to eat or use the restroom. She'd answered in the negative every time.

"Wish she would have let me fly her to Grand Rapids," Rick said. "Would have made it a much quicker trip."

Tom shook his head. "She wasn't kidding when she said she was terrified of small planes. She's no fan of big ones either, but those don't seem to affect her in the same way as small ones. I don't know why. I'm not sure she knows either."

"I'd rather fly than take a boat out this time of year. That dark, icy water is what scares me."

Tom motioned toward the living room. "Want to come in and sit for a while?"

Hallie answered, "No. We'd better get on home. I've got a few festival things to handle."

The Christmas festival. Tom hadn't given it any thought all day. And now, he dreaded next Saturday. He'd imagined himself with Ariel at the festival. He'd imagined watching her have fun. To see that smile blossom. To hear her laughter. He'd pictured her giving out the writing contest award and speaking words of encouragement to all the young writers. He'd imagined her delight in the fireworks after dark. And he'd thought a lot about kissing her under the mistletoe hanging from the arch of the gazebo.

Would he ever kiss Ariel Highbridge again?

The heaviness in his chest grew worse.

"Give us a call if you need anything else," Rick said. "We're here to help."

"Thanks. I appreciate it."

Rick and Hallie walked out into the night, closing the door behind them.

Tom drew a breath to steady himself, then looked down at Shauna and forced a smile. "Are you hungry?"

"No. Miss Hallie fixed me dinner. She said she didn't know how late you'd be."

"Guess I'll have leftover spaghetti."

"I'll sit with you, Dad. Okay?"

"Sure, Peanut. You're my favorite company."

In the kitchen, he took a bowl from the fridge and spooned noodles onto a plate, followed by a generous amount of meat sauce. After covering the food with a paper towel, he put the plate into the microwave and turned it on. Minutes later, he sat at the table with the plate of hot spaghetti before him. He stared at it, twirled it with his fork, but he couldn't make himself eat.

He was scared. He was scared that Ariel wouldn't come back to the island. She'd probably taken everything of importance with her. There might not be any reason for her to return to Sanctuary. She could have Gwyneth ship it to her later.

I should've told her I loved her.

Did she know already? Did she feel the same? He couldn't be sure. And if her mom's health was bad, if the treatment lasted for months, maybe she would forget him. Maybe the feelings they'd shared would never have a chance to mature, to become more. Maybe . . .

God, this hurts. I know it's selfish of me, to think about myself and what I want at a time like this while Ariel's so worried about her mom. But I'm afraid of what I might lose. Help me walk through this with integrity. Help me to walk in Your way and not my own.

CHAPTER 28

It was almost ten o'clock on Thursday morning when the landline phone started ringing. Ariel's mom exchanged glances with her husband and daughter, then rose from the kitchen table and went to pick up the handset from the wall phone.

"Hello . . . Yes, this is Patricia Sherman . . . Yes . . . No . . . I'm sorry?" She collapsed onto a nearby chair. "You're sure?"

Ariel shot to her feet, pulse racing.

"Yes . . . Yes, of course . . . No, no questions . . . Thank you. I appreciate it. Thank you so much . . . Yes, I'll hold."

"Mom?"

Wes moved to stand beside her mom, placing his hand on her shoulder.

Mom held up a finger, silently asking them to wait until she finished. What else could they do?

"Yes, I'm here . . . Yes, I have that link . . . Of course. I'll call if I have any questions . . . Thank you." Mom lowered the handset to her lap. Then she raised her eyes, first looking at Wes, then at Ariel. "It isn't cancer."

A tiny cry escaped Ariel's throat as she dropped to her chair, much as her mom had done moments before.

"Wes." Her mom took his hand. "It isn't cancer."

Tears blinded Ariel. "Thank You, Jesus," she whispered through a tight throat.

"Amen," Wes said.

"Yes, thank You, Jesus." Her mom stood, allowing herself to be enfolded in Wes's arms.

After a period of silence, Ariel asked, "Now what?"

"Nothing, really. I have a link where I can see the test results. Which I imagine will mean nothing to me. Except possibly where it says 'negative' or something like it. But I . . . I just need to keep my next mammogram appointment in a year, as scheduled. No further follow-up unless I have concerns."

Ariel had to blink back another wave of tears. "Oh, Mom. I'm so thankful. So thankful."

"Me, too." Her mom returned to the table and sat near Ariel. "I should be angry with Wes for telling you and making you worry."

"No, you shouldn't. I'm glad he told me. I wanted to be with you."

Mom arched an eyebrow. "I know how much you hate to fly."

"Well, there is that."

"And now you'll need to get on another plane and fly to Michigan again."

Ariel's heart fluttered and her stomach tumbled.

"Christmas is only a week away. I'm here now. I should stay."

"But you would rather spend Christmas with Tom and his daughter." Mom leaned forward. "Wouldn't you?"

She tried to shake her head and couldn't. "Mom, you and I were both feeling bad about being apart for Christmas. Now I'm home. I should stay."

Her mom cast a look in Wes's direction, one that he apparently understood. "Excuse me," he said. "I've got some calls to make." He left the kitchen, and the sound of a closing door deeper in the house soon followed.

"Ariel, listen to me. I loved the surprise of seeing you on Monday night. I love that you wanted to be with me when it seemed the news could be bad. I do. I'm grateful to your friends in Sanctuary who did everything they could to get you here. But honey—" She took Ariel's right hand and pressed it between both of hers. "Listen to me. I've watched you and listened to you over the last three days. I can tell what you feel for Tom and Shauna. For goodness sake, I've already started to love them myself, and we haven't even met."

"Mom—"

"If this cancer scare has reminded me of anything, it's this. Life is short. We aren't guaranteed next month or next year. We aren't guaranteed a next breath. That's all in the Lord's hands. But while we're here on this earth, we need to embrace the life He's given us. We need to love the people He puts into our lives. And from everything I've seen and heard, God's put two very special people into your life, and they're waiting for you on Sanctuary Island."

Wouldn't that make her a terrible daughter, if she wanted to be with Tom and Shauna and would leave her mom only a few days before Christmas in order to be with them?

As if hearing Ariel's thoughts, her mom squeezed her hand again. "I know you love me, sweetheart. There's never been a moment in my life when I've doubted that. But you are a grown woman and you deserve a life apart from me. You deserve a good man, and from everything you've told me, Tom Fuller is just that. You deserve a family, and I think you may have already found a daughter to get one started." She shook her head before Ariel could. "Yes, I know I could be jumping the gun, but life is full of risks. Sometimes we have to take them." She leaned back, letting go of Ariel. "And didn't you promise you would be at the festival? Aren't you supposed to give out an award for writing or something?"

"I was supposed to."

"You still could."

Ariel looked at the clock on the kitchen wall. "I was lucky to get a flight home on such short notice. It's even closer to Christmas now. There might not be a seat available. And the weather there was supposed to turn cold again. Frigid even. There'll be more ice on the lake. It might be impossible for me to get there."

"There will be ways to get you there if God wants it, and if you're willing to trust Him."

She thought of Tom, of his arms around her, of him holding her and kissing her. She remembered the sound of his voice as he'd said, *"It'll be okay, Ariel. You'll see."*

And it was okay. Mom was fine, and she was encouraging Ariel to pursue her own path.

"Don't worry about anything else," Tom had said. *"We'll get you to your mom."*

He'd done everything he could to help her. He'd kept his word. He'd arranged for the boat that could take her to the mainland. He'd borrowed the truck Rick kept in Havensport to drive her to Grand Rapids so she wouldn't have to fly even one leg on a small commuter plane. He'd done whatever he could to help her when she'd been in need. And he'd done it all because he loved her. She'd seen that in his eyes. She'd known it in her own heart even longer.

True, he hadn't said he loved her. But wasn't love a verb? Wasn't love shown by what a person did more than by what was said? Wasn't that the kind of hero she loved to write about?

"Mom, if I can, I'd love to make it home to Sanctuary in time for the festival."

With Scruffy on a leash at his side, Tom stood with other members of the community, watching the ice sculptors work their magic with little chisels, tiny hammers, and bottles of water. Thanks to another cold front plus snowfall in mid-week, the conditions were perfect for this event. In fact, it was a good thing Ariel made it off the island when she did. Taking any boat out today would have been sheer madness with the ice thickening as fast as it was.

"Hey, there." Hallie stepped up beside him, slipping her arm through his. "You enjoying the festival?"

He glanced at her. "You want the truth?"

"Of course."

"Not much."

"Sorry. Haven't heard from Ariel again?"

"Not since her text on Thursday morning. Her mom was still waiting for the results. Do you suppose they haven't heard yet? The waiting is the hardest part, I think."

It could be that he wasn't anywhere close to Ariel's top priority at the moment. And that possibility stung, even if he fully understood why it could be true.

Hallie answered, "I have a feeling you'll hear from her soon."

"Hope you're right." He glanced around. "Where's Rick?"

"He had to make a last minute flight over to the mainland. I expect him back any time now." Hallie released his arm. "What about Shauna? Where's she?"

"She and Lily wanted to compete in the snowshoe races." He looked at his watch. "I'd better get over there to see how it goes. Care to join me?"

"I would love to. Thanks." She bent over and gave Scruffy a scratch behind the ear. "Hey there, boy. How you doing?"

Scruffy stood and wagged his tail in response, and when Tom and Hallie started walking, the dog went to the end of his leash, eagerly pulling toward a destination he couldn't know.

Most years, Tom took pleasure in seeing the year-round residents fill up the town square and the streets connecting with it. He enjoyed the Christmas festival for many reasons. He loved seeing couples walking hand-in-hand. He loved the laughter filling the air. He loved hearing the Merry Christmas greetings exchanged and the music playing from the gazebo. He loved the faces reddened by the cold. He loved the look of anticipation in the children's eyes.

But this year . . .

Tom, Hallie, and Scruffy joined other spectators on one side of the street that served as the track for the races. He leaned forward and looked toward the starting line. He couldn't see Shauna among the kids and adults milling about.

"I thought the first race was just kids around Shauna's age," he said to no one in particular.

"Oh, I think there was a last minute change," Hallie answered. "The first race is a team event with one adult and one child in each team. They have to race with locked arms."

"Really?" He glanced at Hallie. "How come Shauna didn't come get me? She'd want me to race with her." Maybe she'd looked for him and couldn't find him. He cringed. That would disappoint her, and she was already feeling enough of that emotion because of Ariel's absence.

"Oh, look!" Hallie said, excitement in her voice. "They're about to start."

He turned toward the starting line again, his gaze searching for his daughter. He found her just as the starting bell rang. A half second later, he looked at the woman whose arm was linked with Shauna's. But that couldn't be. It looked like—

"Ariel?"

Hallie shouted. "Go, Shauna, go! Keep going, Ariel!"

Rick appeared behind Hallie, placing both hands on her shoulders. "Look at them go. They're gonna win."

If Tom's brain had been working, he would have registered the moment Ariel and Shauna broke through the bright yellow ribbon. If he'd been able to think straight, he might have laughed as woman and girl toppled over into the snow amid cheers and shouts.

"Ariel?"

Rick slapped Tom on the back. "You've got a couple of champions there, my friend. In more ways than one."

Tom blinked as the fog in his head began to clear. "Why is she here? Her mom… How did Ariel get here?"

"I flew her here."

"Flew her? In *your* plane?" His gaze shot to the finish line. "But she's afraid of small planes. Seriously afraid. I saw her face when I suggested it. Her terror is real."

"It is, indeed. But even her terror couldn't hold up against her determination to be with you and Shauna today."

Tom looked at his friend, still not quite believing.

"You'd better go congratulate them," Rick said, grinning.

Tom took a breath. "Thanks. More than I can say."

"Get going."

Tom set off toward the finish line where Vicky Williams was currently placing a ribbon and medal around Shauna's neck. By the time he reached them, Ariel had her award too.

"Ariel. You're here."

She smiled at him, and her eyes seemed to sparkle with joy.

"I didn't know you'd be here. I never expected—"

"Mom loved the surprise of seeing me so much, I rather hoped you would feel the same if I surprised you with my return. Rick and Hallie helped make it happen."

"I am surprised." He handed Scruffy's leash to Shauna, then took hold of Ariel's upper arms. "But your mom," he added softly.

"She's fine. It isn't cancer."

"Thank God."

"Yes."

"You flew with Rick?" The wonder of it washed over him again. "In his plane."

"It was the only way to reach the island before another thaw. I couldn't wait that long to get to you."

"To me?"

Her smile shone even brighter. "To you and Shauna."

He drew her closer. She tipped her head back, looking up at him, and he wondered if it was possible to drown in her gaze.

In a stage whisper, Shauna said, "Do you need me to go get some mistletoe, Dad?"

He laughed as he glanced at his daughter, who stood right beside them, staring up with the happiest look he could remember seeing on her freckled face in a very long time. It perfectly mirrored the feelings in his heart. "Peanut, there is no mistletoe required." He returned his gaze to Ariel. "Miss Highbridge, in case you don't know it already, I love you."

"I suspected, Mr. Fuller, but I'm so glad to hear you say

the words. And in case you have any doubts, I love you too. The kind of love I like to write about but never expected to find."

Shauna said loudly, "This is when you're supposed to kiss her, Dad."

"I know, kiddo." His hands came up to cradle Ariel's face. "I know."

He lowered his mouth and kissed her as instructed. The kiss was long and slow and deep. He kissed her, not caring who saw him do so. The whole island would know about it soon enough anyway. He was fairly certain it was the kind of kiss every hero in a romance novel should bestow upon his heroine.

But he would ask Ariel about that later.

EPILOGUE

One year later

The Sanctuary Island annual Christmas festival was in full swing. The town square and surrounding streets teemed with people. Ice sculptors were perfecting their creations. The snowshoe races would begin on East Third in about fifteen minutes. The barbershop quartet sang in the gazebo, their harmonies filling the air with merriment and good cheer. Tiny lights sparkled in the trees. An abundance of food was set out on tables around the square.

Standing near the gazebo, an arm around Ariel's shoulders, Tom looked at the milling crowd, and happiness washed over him. These people—the ones he could see and even those out of his sight—represented so many of the reasons why he loved living on this island, even in winter. He took particular notice of the newer couples in the crowd. There must have been something in the island's water supply the previous year, because he could see more than one newlywed couple in the town square today. He'd counted them already. Six in all, including himself and Ariel.

There was Nate and Harper Hawthorn. Tom and Nate shared a common past, having both lost their first wives. But God had blessed them both with a second chance at love, and now the Hawthorns were expecting a baby brother or sister for little Emma, and she was the happiest little girl on the island!

Off in the distance, he noted Taylor Everest—only the second Christmas festival the man had attended in over a decade. Taylor still held himself apart from the crowd of island natives, but that was Taylor's nature. Quiet, kept to himself. But now Taylor Everest was quietly content rather than silently unhappy. The main reason for the change stood at his side, his wife Sonora.

Not far away from Taylor, Tom spotted Chloe and Derrick Webster standing near the food tables. No doubt Chloe was making sure everything she'd prepared was just right. Everyone knew she was a perfectionist when it came to her food. Everyone also knew how much those two former adversaries loved each other.

Tom laughed softly as he watched Chloe slap Derrick's hand away from one of the food trays. Then his gaze traveled on.

Not far from the Websters, he saw the new Dr. and Mrs. Brunswick in a lively conversation with another couple. Married in the fall, Colton and Angelica had already overcome so much. It was heartwarming to see the once-reserved doctor embracing life on the island, all thanks to Angelica's infectious enthusiasm and the town's welcoming arms.

At the cookie decorating table, Jo Fletcher—Knox now, Tom corrected himself—stood behind her daughter, Sam, as the little girl applied a liberal helping of sprinkles to her cookie. Beckett Knox walked over carrying three steaming cups of cocoa and set them on the table before examining Sam's handiwork. He reached for the sprinkle container and tipped it upside down over the cookie, adding to the colorful hill on top of it. Jo lunged to stop him, laughing as Beckett used the occasion to wrap his arms around her and plant a kiss on her forehead.

Tom's attention returned to Ariel. His bride of six months was as beautiful in her puffy winter coat, her nose and cheeks red from the cold, as she'd been walking down the church aisle in a gorgeous white gown on their wedding day. Although it was more traditional to wed in the bride's hometown, Ariel had chosen to be married in Sanctuary in their community church, Shauna as her flower girl and Gwyneth and Hallie as her bridesmaids. And of course, Ariel's mom and Wes had flown in for the occasion.

Their wedding day couldn't have been more perfect as far as Tom was concerned. And pretty much every day that had followed it had been perfect too.

ARIEL LOOKED UP AT TOM, and his smile warmed her far more than the coat, hat, and boots she wore. In a million years, she couldn't have dreamed, when she'd accepted

ROBIN LEE HATCHER

Gwyneth's offer to use her home on this island, that it would bring her to a forever kind of love with this wonderful man.

Ariel's own happiness had spilled into her writing. Right after the start of the new year, she'd written her next Regency novel, filled with love and romance—and a hero who looked, acted, and spoke suspiciously like Tom Fuller. She'd managed to turn in the manuscript a full two months before the due date. No extension required. Then —still happy and inspired—she'd returned to her contemporary story, the one destined for the general market. She'd written it in record time. The words had seemed to pour out of her onto the laptop screen with little effort on her part. Then Michael Prescott had done exactly as he'd said he would. The agent optioned her manuscript to a film production company even before she'd signed a publishing contract, although that had followed soon after.

Still, as wonderful as that all was, she'd found her real joy and contentment as Tom's wife and Shauna's mom. Not to mention Scruffy's obedience coach.

"Ready to head over to the snowshoe races?" Tom asked, looking at her in a way that made her go all soft inside.

"I'm ready."

"Are you sorry you didn't agree to race with Shauna again? I mean, you two were the medalists last year."

She laughed. "No. I'm good with watching this time."

Tonight she would tell him why she preferred to stand on the sidelines rather than risk a hard fall in the snow. Tonight she would tell him their little family was going to grow from three to four in about seven months.

As they turned toward East Third Street, Ariel happened to look up and notice the mistletoe hanging from the eaves of the gazebo. "Look." She pointed. "Does that suggest anything to you?"

He followed her gesture with his eyes, then returned his gaze to her. "Oh, Mrs. Fuller. Haven't you learned by now that no mistletoe is required?"

And then, much to her satisfaction, he proved it.

If you enjoyed *Wishing for Mistletoe*, please take a moment to leave a review on Amazon, Goodreads, and/or BookBub. Word of mouth is the best way you can tell an author you liked her story.

And if you haven't read all the books in the Love on Sanctuary Shores series (especially if the epilogue of *Wishing for Mistletoe* made you wonder about those five additional newlywed couples Tom notices during the festival), be sure to read the other books now. Available on Amazon in Kindle, print, and KU. If you are reading the ebook copy, you can click the image of the series covers, and it will take you to the right page on Amazon.

Tumbling into Tomorrow by Juliette Duncan
Fighting for Her Heart by Tara Grace Ericson
Surrendering to Love by Kristen M. Fraser
Running into Forever by Jennifer Rodewald
Trusting His Promise by Valerie M. Bodden
Wishing for Mistletoe by Robin Lee Hatcher

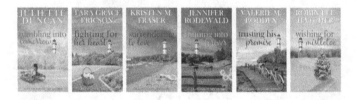

Don't forget to sign up for Robin's monthly email newsletter at https://robinleehatcher.com/newsletter-sign-up/. Subscribers receive a free ebook copy of her historical romance, *Speak to Me of Love,* and US subscribers are entered every month in a drawing to win two paperback novels.

ABOUT THE AUTHOR

Robin Lee Hatcher is the best-selling author of over 90 books. Her well-drawn characters and heartwarming stories of faith, courage, and love have earned her both critical acclaim and the devotion of readers. Her numerous awards include the Christy Award for Excellence in Christian Fiction, the RITA® Award for Best Inspirational Romance, Romantic Times Career Achievement Awards for Americana Romance and for Inspirational Fiction, the Carol Award, the 2011 Idahope Writer of the Year, and Lifetime Achievement Awards from both Romance Writers of America® (2001) and American Christian Fiction Writers (2014).

When not writing, Robin enjoys being with her family, spending time in the beautiful Idaho outdoors, Bible art journaling, reading books that make her cry, watching romantic movies, knitting, and decorative planning. A mother and grandmother, Robin makes her home on the outskirts of Boise, sharing it with a demanding Papillon dog and a persnickety tuxedo cat.

Learn more about Robin and her books by visiting her website at robinleehatcher.com

You can also find out more by joining her on Facebook, X, and/or Instagram.

facebook.com/robinleehatcher
x.com/robinleehatcher
instagram.com/robinleehatcher

ALSO BY ROBIN LEE HATCHER

The Perfect Life

Speak to Me of Love

Trouble in Paradise

Another Chance to Love You

Bundle of Joy

The British Are Coming series

To Enchant a Lady's Heart

To Marry an English Lord

To Capture a Mountain Man (early 2025)

Boulder Creek Romances

Even Forever

All She Ever Dreamed

The Coming to America series

Dear Lady

Patterns of Love

In His Arms

Promised to Me

Where the Heart Lives series

Belonging

Betrayal

Beloved

Books set in Kings Meadow

A Promise Kept

Love Without End

Whenever You Come Around

I Hope You Dance

Keeper of the Stars

Books set in Thunder Creek

You'll Think of Me

You're Gonna Love Me

The Sisters of Bethlehem Springs series

A Vote of Confidence

Fit to Be Tied

A Matter of Character

Legacy of Faith series

Who I Am with You

Cross My Heart

How Sweet It Is

For a full list of books along with blurbs, reviews, and awards, visit robinleehatcher.com

Printed in the USA
CPSIA information can be obtained
at www.ICGtesting.com
LVHW040520231024
794545LV00006B/124